Strange Flight

Edited by
Leonie Skye

Contributions by
Victoria Feistner, Yvette Franklin,
Timothy Lamoureux, David Preyde,
Leonie Skye, Lisa Timpf

ELM BOOKS, 2019

Laramie, Wyoming

Strange Flight edited by Leonie Skye
Copyright © 2019 by Elm Books

Paperback ISBN: 978-1-941614-30-3
E-Format ISBN: 978-1-941614-31-0
Print Edition

Elm Books
1175 State Highway 130
Laramie, WY 82070
(elm-books.com)

Cover design: Lottie Patterson
Anhinga photo credit: William Korn
Copy editing: Masha Sten-Clanton and Alison Quaggin Harkin
Text formatting: BB eBooks

Table of Contents

Foreword

When you get to the very end of the line—the end of freedom, of life support systems, of the world as we know it—how do you cheat fate and keep going? What mysterious portals might open onto new dimensions, what previously invisible corners be turned, what fantastical opportunities appear? And what physical states or moral convictions, what certainties about yourself and your world must be left behind as a consequence? In Elm Books' second science fiction anthology featuring protagonists with disabilities, six new stories probe the idea of life-changing escape.

Buckle your seat belts and prepare for *Strange Flight*.

Leonie Skye, September 2019

Music of the Spheres

by Victoria Feistner

THE WAVE-SKIMMER COASTED to the edges of the system as the front of the shockwave diminished, washing out as calculated.

The computer gently woke Emmen. Lights grew from points as tiny as fireflies to soft pre-dawn glows, while the computer dried the drip and Emmen's taxed, too-human endocrine system began to pulse and ripple—consciousness being a by-product of the lack of narcotics.

The *intended* effect was peaceful dozing followed by natural waking—a simulated Sunday morning in space.

Instead, a tight spasm in Emmen's leg jolted her painfully awake. A brief, woozy moment was spent identifying the wall across from her webbing, and then she was at full alertness. Not a lazy weekend waking; more like a bleary, dizzy startlement, as if she was late for a morning meeting.

As the haze cleared, she remembered too clearly: she was alone. She fought the pain of another spasm and worked her right arm free from the harness. She groped for the controls to the drips. Pain relief surged down the lines, and the sudden freedom coaxed a sigh from her, as she closed her eyes and snuggled back in to try and awaken properly this time.

IN HER EARLY academic days Emmen had abhorred sleeping past an alarm—indicative of laziness—but age, perspective, and constant pain had mellowed her. She still wasn't anyone's idea of laid-back. But as she struggled to free herself from the showering unit, she reflected on the realization that her actions no longer mattered to people. Their minds were made; all the facts tallied. She was no longer around to change their opinions of her. She pulled herself up via the top edge of the door and dragged her protesting left leg manually over the spill-lip.

It's gotten worse while I was sleeping. But increasing her doseage would impair mental functions. And that she would not tolerate.

"Coordinates." Her voice cracked, raspy and worn.

The computer displayed a diagram on the inset panel closest to her, although far enough away that she had to squint. *Still out of range of the outer planets. Good.* She trusted her calculations, but there was so much in deep space that could go wrong, and she did not want to go back into stasis to try again. Or spend more time awake amid worsening symptoms.

Perching on the pull-out console stool, she dried herself while laboriously keying the launch commands for the beacons with one hand. Once the count-down began, she committed herself fully to the toweling. Outmoded and inefficient, sure, but the vigorous massage tingled her toes, and the jumping muscles of her legs calmed briefly, warmed by circulation. Goosebumps tickled across her skin—oh, a joy to feel—as the microvents scattered throughout the skimmer did their duties.

The amplification beacons deployed. First a shudder rocked the ship—Emmen dropped the towel and grabbed onto a support railing—turning into a much more violent shaking as the various engines fired, a series of percussive shock waves buffeting from both sides, rippling past and through each other.

She gritted her teeth and tightened her grip, trying to keep her neck steady. Her left leg kicked out uselessly, but she fought the spasms in her arms to hold on.

At last, the rocking slowed enough that the stabilizers could once again cope and the skimmer stilled. Breathing in small gasps, she unclenched herself, prying white-knuckled fingers from the railing, and staggered to her feet, all joy from the massage gone, the towel left in a damp heap. She had two days for all the beacons to be deployed so that they could reach position above their target planets. One day before they began relaying sound. In the meantime, she needed her bunk and her meds.

✦   ✦   ✦

EMMEN SPENT THE next two days in a semi-aware state, punctuated by moments of pain-filled lucidity or drug-induced sleep. The auto-deployment suffered no setbacks.

On the evening of the third day post-hibernation, she read updated medical status reports; there had been significant deterioration throughout the voyage. So much for her specialist's claim that the hibernation would prove beneficial.

Being right was no comfort.

Her back, where the chair's acrylic fabric clung, grew sweaty and itchy, and she scratched absent-mindedly. A sudden contraction in her tendon caused her fingers to clench in reaction, gouging a swift rent in her skin. She hadn't thought to trim her fingernails. Hissing, she drew her still-twitching hand away, the muscles roiling, her nerves yelling in consternation.

"Please lower cabin temperature by two degrees," she instructed the skimmer's computer, keeping her voice low. And then: "How much longer for Beacon 5 to reach its projected destination?"

A display flickered into being, a diagram of the system showing the two stars, three planets, and the current positions of all the beacons.

Soon, then.

No point in going to sleep if she had to run calibrations.

Stretching and relaxing the fingers of both hands, Emmen waited for a calm moment to key a command. On the overhead display, the diagram of the HCB93 system was replaced by a video, the recording date almost—save one day—exactly two Terran years ago.

"We are gathered here," the speaker said solemnly, her shoulders drooping, her head heavy, "to say goodbye to our friend and colleague Wen Li…"

Emmen watched, expressionless, the memorial's transcript already memorized, engraved deep within.

IT PLAYED ON a loop even as Beacon 5's telemetry reached the skimmer's sensors. Background noise, losing out to Emmen's focus out the window at the ever-shining binary suns. At the edge of the system, the stars were brighter than their far-flung cousins but dim enough to view through unshaded glass.

Spasms—tiny flutterings, this time—were ignored. Time slowed. The memorial drifted even further from her conscious perception as she stared at the center of the HCB93 system.

As a small child gazing through Mars' thin atmosphere with her telescope, she'd wondered. As an adult and a researcher at the university, she'd theorized. It had taken a lifetime to find this system, out of the billions on record.

She should have had more decades to search, but even as a child she knew her timeline was swift. She had to maintain focus.

Dominic said she'd been lucky to find the system when she did. Outwardly she'd insisted to him that it was a culmination of a lifetime of work, even if that lifetime was short. Inwardly she agreed with him; after all, her broken genes were a kind of luck as well. One sort might as well cancel out the other.

Eventually—how long had that light been flashing? That indicator beeping?—Emmen's sense of self contracted, and awareness of her surroundings drifted in. Shaking her head to stay focused, she keyed up the new data. The final beacon was ready—no mishaps reported. She activated the test and calibration subroutine, careful to turn the speakers to mute, even going so far as to shut down the memorial halfway.

"… it was always Wen Li's dream to…" The image darkened, and for the first time since Emmen had first watched the recording, tears stung at the corners of her eyes, and the heavens grew blurry. For the first time since she had left Mars, the stars twinkled.

DECADES OF FOCUS and rumination. How old had she been when the idea first came to her? After her initial diagnosis, certainly. So, seven. Eight, perhaps. She'd always been firm in her decision. And yet, Emmen vividly recalled the expressions on the faces of her colleagues as she informed them of her plan, as she terminated or delegated her other projects at the

University.

I know you are facing a tough road, Dominic had said, his face slack with… what? Disappointment? Sadness? Horror? *But is this the right way to go about it? About the…?*

"… We are gathered here today…" the recording intruded on Emmen's recollections.

The grief, you mean, Dominic? She had momentarily enjoyed the consternation on his face at her detachment. He'd always made fun of her ability to stay so calm. But he wasn't laughing, just staring at her, hands clenched. *Isn't the grieving process different for everyone?*

"… much beloved by her students and the faculty, renowned for her research, her love for the cosmos and its eternal surprises and mysteries…"

This isn't grief!

It is. But a grief so old it means nothing any more.

Maybe she should have told him sooner. Given him more time to process.

Oddly enough, she thought, alone in the wave skimmer, staring at her reflection in the viewport, it had been grief and time she'd been trying to spare him.

IT HAD TAKEN her years of combing records, of compiling data—almost all her off-hours at the university, plus snatched moments between astrophysics lectures, seminars, and labs.

But she knew the probability of its existence in an infinite universe, as well as the small chance of its being among the severely *finite* number of systems that humans had catalogued in the scant centuries of stargazing and starlistening.

Her dream might have stayed beyond humanity's current reach, but then she located a good candidate: PSR-HCB93, a small, useless, unnamed system, its rocky inner planets—if they had even existed—vaporized in the novas that had produced PSR-HCB93-A's and PSR-HCB93-B's current incarnations. Three gassy, titanic outer planets were left miraculously intact.

And even more miraculously vibrating in harmony. Singing to the universe.

Which was, after all, infinite.

"… a legacy of research, of knowledge. But to her friends and acquaintances, this passionate, consummate academician displayed a sentimental streak with her love of music…"

Emmen scoffed each time at that point in the playback. Sentimental? Ridiculous! Popular music was sentimental, perhaps. Even ancient music. Perhaps the whole sphere of human music production could be so considered, tainted as it was by the imperfections of its biological creators.

She had been looking for something more, something pure—mathematically perfect—distinct from humanity with all its disappointments.

And in PSR-HCB93, she had found it. Mere months after

the terminal diagnosis was official. Maybe Dom was right, and it was luck.

She made the arrangements, tied up her loose ends, left everything as neat and as organized as she could. She'd anticipated the day for so long that she was swift and methodical, shocking many. Her colleagues knew of her chronic illness, but none knew how degenerative it was, how long she'd known it would kill her, and how painfully. She never spoke of it if she could avoid doing so.

But it was always in the back of her mind, counting down.

She hadn't intended to view the memorial—she'd planned to be long out of broadcast range by then. But Dominic—the only one to whom she'd told the truth of her private research—had somehow arranged for a delay in her departure, so her skimmer was still in range to receive the transmission of the recording.

Perhaps he had meant it as a goodbye.

Perhaps he had hoped it would make her change her mind.

On first watching the recording she had broken down and wept—for the first time since her final diagnosis. For the life now over.

She wished that she had been able to tell Dominic that he was right, in a way—maybe some components of grief and loss were never truly over. But even if she sent him a note, he would never receive it. The signal would take years to hit Mars, even if anyone was listening.

As the lights brightened for the last time, Emmen struggled

with the sleeping webbing, her weak muscles and broken nerves fighting her will. And winning.

For now.

EMMEN CONSIDERED HER wardrobe. Originally she'd planned to wear her researcher's uniform, which had so long defined her sense of self, but these past few days she'd reconsidered. She wasn't that person any more. Hadn't been, since that last day on Mars. Instead she dressed in a civilian one-piece, thin and clinging, made to fit under a Martian exosuit, decorated in the colors of her youth, a present from before she left for Olympia City and Mars University.

She made her way to the bridge at the front of the skimmer, the microvents along the stuttering, staggering walk raising strips of tingling gooseflesh. She took a modicum of pleasure in the sensation, although not in the accompanying flashes and stabs of pain. Today she was off the narcotics entirely: she was no longer afraid.

More important, she wanted her full faculties open to her, all edges undulled.

As she sat in the chair, trembling from the exertion, she lowered the temperature again, and with excruciating effort at precision, commanded the computer to begin her program. This was the culmination of her life's passion, of carefully executed plans—and the defiance of her disease and its outcome.

The lights dimmed, and she leaned back. A light-based schematic drew itself around her, the lines glowing faintly in the darkness, showing A, B, their planets, and the positions of all the beacons.

She reached a trembling finger to tap at the largest dot, which represented PSR-HCB93-A. At once, the skimmer filled with sound: a steady beat, the frequency greatly diminished so as to be heard by human ears, but the star's own sound all the same.

PSR-HCB93-A was a medium-sized radio pulsar. B, its smaller companion, was *also* a pulsar. A pair of starhearts— remnants from twin supernovae, throwing off radio waves instead of the more energetic gamma or x-ray pulses.

A binary pair was rare, but not astoundingly so. Where PSR-HCB93 Alpha and Beta became exceptional was that together their cosmic beats, when heard by a human, were pleasing.

They were music.

She tapped the third beacon, near the innermost planet, and its sound joined its parents inside the skimmer. A deep rumble, caused by movements within the planet, its magneto-sphere, and the shock waves of the nearby binary against its atmosphere. All the planets—she tapped Beacons 4 and 5 in quick succession—were, through lucky happenstance, undestroyed by the supernovae that produced the pulsars. All produced rumbles—all planets did—but these five sources, in this one system, barely noted in a surveyor's log a century prior, came together in harmony.

To a human, of course. Other species might find PSR-HCB93 unremarkable. Maybe some humans would as well; the melody, such as it was, was very simple.

But to Emmen, it was beautiful.

She increased the volume until the bass reverberated against her breastbone, so that she could feel the pulse of the stars within her own flesh. Leaning all the way back, she closed her eyes, absorbing the music of the universe, the eerie wavering harmonies, the twin pulses.

Her muscles could not relax as her mind did. They twitched and shrieked, clenched and released so as to bring tears to her eyes. But Emmen refused to give in.

She was choosing her own path through the heavens. Her genes had chosen the length of the road, but they did not determine her route. The choices she had made had led her here, one fork after another, but the roads not taken didn't matter any longer. Pain would not drown her; her determination had won.

She blindly reached, shaking, to a drawer underneath the console. Unlatching it was hard—to focus on such a menial task when there was such simple, perfect, eternal music that cried out for her undivided attention.

But she had to do this.

✦ ✦ ✦

EMMEN WITHDREW THE metal canister, keeping her grip tight. The exertion was torturous. She brought it to her chest, resting until she recovered. Opening the top took both hands and steadying breaths. It was a memento from childhood, an old-fashioned money-bank a grandparent had brought back from Earth. She'd kept spare parts for her telescope in it, bringing it with her on every excursion out to the red hills. She'd left behind much when she left home, but she'd taken the canister and her one-piece as reminders of her innocence.

Dominic had surprised her by getting the canister repaired and engraved when she made chair all those years ago, when they were still together. He was so tender-hearted, Dom, so stubbornly sentimental. But then perhaps she too had such a streak; after all, she had used the tin for many years after they'd parted, storing things of one kind or another in it. She wondered what he'd think to know she'd brought it with her. She supposed the knowledge would have brought him some small comfort.

And now, as she prized it open, the syringe fell into her lap, the tip of the needle pricking—but not breaking—her bare skin.

She relaxed, resting, twitching, spasms from the effort rippling along her extremities. She was so tired, so ready for sleep and more ever-failing meds, but what would that bring? Only tomorrow; only the same decision. But with a greater chance of worsening pain.

The steady rhythm of PSR-HCB93 rolled around her, through her, and reminded Emmen of how large and impossible, how immeasurably beautiful her universe was, and how small and useless she was within it. An animate collection of molecules, no different in truth from the inanimate, far larger collections that sang all around her. That would sing forever— or long enough.

She swiftly pressed the syringe deep into her thigh, wary of a spasm in her grip that could send the needle flying away from her.

Her muscles began to truly quiet, while she lay listening to the music of the spheres, her dream of a sublime last moment realized.

The tin dropped to the floor, unheard, rolling until it came to rest, its worn inscription face up in the starlight.

To Wen Li Emmen, Mars U, 2315

As your favorite philosopher once said:
> *There is geometry in the humming of the strings;*
> *there is music in the spacing of the spheres.*
> *Congratulations on making Chair.*

Love,
Dom

And the sounds of heaven filled the cabin, and the skimmer drifted on.

The Darkness of Goo

by Yvette Franklin

SLOWLY, NANI CAME back to consciousness. She could see nothing. She had been at the console piloting *The Blink* to the Luhman 16 AB system. The dim gas giants had been growing larger in the bridge-deck screen when a light had sliced through the ship. Now, nothing but darkness. What was outside her suit was not normal air, not even the normal vacuum that she had played in since she was a small child. What surrounded her was heavier than air. Denser. Thicker than water. She was trapped in some strange otherworld jello. She panicked and started to thrash in the goo that engulfed her.

But she could breathe in her suit, so she took a breath and tried to stop thrashing.

It was as dark as her bunk in the *Eliza Clerc*, the home ship where she'd been raised from childhood. The darkness of the *Eliza* had not been bad. She considered it her second memory. Her first memory was a woman and a man giving her to people wearing what she would later know to be space fatigues. The man had hugged her goodbye. The woman had not. When thinking about the event, she could see a very bright background, one that she wasn't sure was light from ordinary planetary daytime, or a city nighttime full of bright lights. Funny that she remembered the light. Because the memories of darkness were memories of her real home. She had been only two and a half when she had been given over to the Spacers. Her mama and da would never tell her what planet had given her to the Space Corps, just that her bio-mother was a eugenicist and couldn't abide a Deaf child. Mama said her biofather had made sure she was given to the Chilmark Consortium, one of the oldest space firms. He had known she should be with a Deaf family. The darkness of her *Eliza* bunk had been scary at first, but that had turned out fine.

She took a deep breath and tried to return to the space she was in, not to let the darkness rip her from the present. She couldn't just accept the darkness: she had to navigate it, find a way to pilot through it.

She felt herself signing her worries into the world. She finger-spelled J-E-L-L-O J-E-L-L-O. J-E-L-L-O. Then she started signing OKAY OKAY OKAY, and FINE FINE FINE. Her fingers moved slowly through the goo, but she could still communicate. Yes, she was an Eyes. Yes, she had been chosen as part of the crew of *The Blink* because of the way she analyzed the things she saw around her. *The Blink* was a sense ship, one of a fleet of small ships sent out to the far reaches of the universe.

They were on a mission to Luhman 16 AB to examine the source of unexplained rhythmic transmissions. *The Blink* had been in the Centauri system when the Captain won the bid for the Luhman contract. Because Nani was not partnered, she'd signed on for a decade contract—going to Luhman and then getting back to the known worlds was going to take a while. What she hadn't counted on was the four years of day-in and day-out traveling at very near light speed to end in a huge bang that had dumped her in this f-ing goo.

Her expertise in the visual realm was how she got her bunk on a sense ship. But what she analyzed was patterns. What did that array of numbers mean? Why did the liquids on a certain planet run red? There had to be patterns beyond the world of vision. The Captain was triple qualified as a Hands, Nose, and Mouth, even if she was Deaf Blind. Olivia was a Mouth and approached the world through taste. Gorilla, *The Blink*'s Hands, had keen touch perception. He'd known whatever this was, wherever they were, was coming way before she could see proof of it.

She could smell nothing in her space suit. Then she realized her suit was not recycling air or working off the bottle. Normal suit info, the ongoing stream of green numbers and short words describing the world just below eye level, was not being transmitted, but her suit didn't feel like it was broken. She had no problems breathing. Her suit was taking air from the environment. She couldn't even feel a filter running. She could not resist. She undid her faceplate and opened her mouth wide and tried to taste. Her tongue barely reached the surrounding goo. Pretty neutral, perhaps slightly salty.

Opening her faceplate made her realize she could breathe through the goo. And the reason she could breathe was that the goo was not jello but a foam or a sponge, air trapped in little bubbles. It must be a sophisticated technology designed to support human life forms because it was too much of a coincidence to be parallel evolution. It certainly was not something she'd come across in her days as a ship kid or as space crew. GOOD, she thought to herself, that was three patterns she recognized. The material was a gooey sponge, it was something unfamiliar to her, and some unknown intelligence had probably developed it. She closed her faceplate.

She stilled her movements. After Eyes, her strongest sense was probably Hands. She was a signer. She used her hands all the time to make sense of her surroundings. She slowly reached her arms out and tried to feel the world. INTERESTING, NEUTRAL BALANCE, she thought as she stretched out. She could feel waves, slight rhythmic waves, buffet her body. MORSE CODE? Both the Captain and Gorilla knew Morse. But she couldn't pinpoint where the movements were coming from. If they were out there, they might be able to find her if she made some waves. She allowed herself the luxury of thrashing. Her arms and legs sliced through the goo, fighting the pressure with every inch. She wasn't panicking, she was attracting attention. Energy released with every kick and slow swipe of her arms through the goo. CAREFUL, DON'T FATIGUE. She stilled her body again, waiting for the ripples she had created to fade, and tried to feel a response, any response.

She was alive, trapped in goo. Logic indicated that her shipmates, the Captain, Olivia, Gorilla, and Janus, Olivia's partner, were most likely alive and trapped as well. Stuck like pieces of bad fruit in an old-fashioned jello salad. Those faint rhythms she felt showed somebody else was around. Sense team members worked together to explore new worlds. If she could connect to her crew, together they could figure out what was going on. They were explorers. This was exactly what they trained for. This was adventure, not disaster. Even though adventures usually had much more to look at: the open vistas of deep space, mountains stretching out far in front of her, even the tall buildings of synthplanet cities reaching into the sky. This was an adventure of her other senses, the ones she did not use as often. An adventure of the heart. That idea bolstered her.

She tried to think of what would be useful. Occasional thrashing to show where she was. She waved her arms and legs again in a rhythmic motion. "S O S," she made her body say in Morse, "S O S." WHAT ELSE USEFUL? She could check her suit functions. No lights anywhere but it still felt like it was protecting her from the world. She turned her head and tried the hydration tube and the nutrient tube. TWO-THUMBS-UP, BOTH WORK. She felt for rips and other damage in her suit. No rips, no damage that she could perceive. Still could feel no vibrations coming closer. NO PANIC, DARKNESS OLD FRIEND, she told herself, trying to believe it.

She started testing the properties of the goo again. *The Blink* was too small to have a pool but her home ship had had a small one. Water play was thought to be good for space kids and the pool served as back-up water storage when needed. Time to try out some old moves. She wrapped herself in a ball and used her arms to somersault forward. The somersault felt slow. Goo was thicker than water. She flipped backwards, and then did a slow pirouette, and somersaulted again with her legs straight in a pike position. The goo did not have the delicious slippery quality of water, but it did offer some of the freedom of movement she had always loved. ONE MORE, she told herself. ONE MORE.

When she stilled her flips and explorations, she could feel movement beyond her, perhaps even coming towards her. Then her leg crashed into something. She had no sense of up or down, but she flipped her body so her hands were near what she kicked. The object she'd bumped into was a pair of hands. Large hands. She bent forward to reach her hands to his. "GORILLA!!" she signed directly to his hand.

"YES!" he signed back. He wasn't a great signer but she had never been happier to see (or not see) him.

"WHATS-UP?" she asked. He responded slowly but clearly in tactile sign that the Captain thought they had been captured by some unknown intelligence, and that they were somehow being observed. Gorilla, known by others as Jacksom, also told her that he was attached to the Captain by a long slender thread. He invited her to follow the thread back to the Captain. She moved her arms around behind him until she could find the thread. She pinched it, and then started swimming back along the thread to the anchor point, back to the Captain.

Finally, she started feeling the weight as the end of the thread grew closer. She got to the end and the Captain tapped her, acknowledging her presence. Nani fell back on formality: "REPORTING FOR DUTY." The Captain, Sali Watson of the Watson Consortium, hugged her.

"HOW YOU, NANI?" asked the Captain.

"OKAY," replied Nani, deeply relieved to be in contact with the Captain's fluent signing again. "NOT LIKE DARK, BUT INTERESTING PLACE."

When Gorilla returned, Nani explained her theories about the goo to her shipmates—that it was a foam or sponge with ordinary atmospheric oxygen and nitrogen imbedded in the matrix.

Gorilla wasn't interested in the goo. What he was interested in was finding Olivia and Janus, which a sensible preoccupation. The Captain said she could feel vibrations and thought it might be Oli or Janus.

Nani took off her glove, to the shock of the Captain and Gorilla, and tried to feel the universe around her. "I-FEEL BUZZ AND I-FEEL WAVES. WAVES FEEL HUMAN," she told both of them with some awkward tactile signing to both of them at once. The Captain theorized that they were in a sphere, and she suspected the buzzes were coming from equidistant points around the sphere. The Captain had a PhD in radio interferometry and explained that the waves she was feeling seemed as if they were trapped in a bubble. Ripples seemed to be emanating from particular points and then back from a surface. The rhythms they had been sent to explore suddenly seemed much more complex than when they set out.

"BUILT. NOT NATURAL," concluded the Captain. Nani shivered. The Captain had expected to find some previously unknown solar interactions as the cause for the rhythms, not real-life extraterrestrial intelligences outside anything previously known. The universe was a big place, but no descendant of Earth had ever met another species as far as either of them knew. Nani ignored the big question to focus on the small and immediate.

"ANY BUZZES DISTINCT?" she asked.

"YES," replied the Captain, "ONE ABOVE MY-HELMET LONG-STEADY BUZZ. ONE I-POINT-TO WITH RIGHT-ARM SHARP FAST BUZZ."

"NAME LONG STEADY UP AND SHARP FAST NORTH?" continued Nani. "LONGITUDE LATITUDE ONLY GIVE EXTERIOR OF-

GLOBE MEASUREMENTS, UP AND NORTH GIVE 3-D MEASURE-MENTS FOR-WHOLE-GLOBE."

"THAT WORKS," replied the Captain. Gorilla didn't seem to quite understand; he was dyslexic and not good at things like spherical coordinates. Nani knew because she'd tried to tutor him in them herself. He caught on quickly once Nani had moved his body so his helmet pointed Up and his arm pointed North. He got it then. He was such a Hands, so reliant on the physical.

Then he went right back to the question of Oli and Janus. "WHICH DIRECTION?" he asked.

Nani had a theory that she confirmed with the Captain and Gorilla. On the ship, Gorilla had probably been about halfway between Nani and the Captain. Nani suggested that they were arrayed in the same relative orientations to one another as they were in the bridge deck of the ship. The Captain had been sitting in the rightmost seat, with Jacksom next to her, manning the guns. Then Nani had been next to him piloting, with Olivia and then Janus next to her. That meant Gorilla needed to retrace the path he had taken to find her. It roughly accorded with the human set of movements down to the southwest of them.

"STAY HERE," he said, controlling male to the end, as he dove into the goo and swam away from them.

Nani was grateful when he left, both because he had a good shot of finding Oli and Janus, and because she and the Captain could now talk shop about the ship and the physics of the situation.

"YOU-KNOW WHERE SHIP?" asked Nani.

"TRYING TO-FEEL SIGNAL BUT NOTHING," responded the Captain. Nani could feel the frustration in the Captain's hands as she conveyed her words.

Nani suddenly had a vision in her head of her, Gorilla, and the Captain exploding out of the ship, and started trying to explain what she thought happened and draw the rays of the explosion on the Captain's hand. The Captain yanked off her gloves so she could feel what Nani was trying to convey.

"YES!" exclaimed the Captain after Nani redrew the ship as the point source of the explosion and the three points representing the three of them. "BUT RAYS NOT FROM LINE, RAYS FROM TRIANGULAR PLANE. BLINK BRIDGE DECK CONSOLE CURVATURE $\sim 1/3 \text{ M}^{-1}$."

"RIGHT!" signed Nani swiftly. "ASSUMING ORTHOGONAL DISTRIBUTION EMANATING-FROM LOCATION-OF-BLINK, SHIP POSITION-IS $(1/3 (X_a + X_b + X_c), 1/3(Y_a + Y_b + Y_c))$."

"YES," replied the Captain. Nani could feel the Captain's fingers twitching as she calculated and had never been so glad to have a boss good at mental mathematics. After a short pause, the Captain replied, "IF WE-BASE COORDINATES ON $\sim$ SWIM TIME AND CURVATURE, CENTROID IS $\sim$ 8 SOL-MINUTES NORTH, 25 SM EAST. WE-DON'T KNOW Z = HEIGHT COORDINATE BUT HAVE PLACE TO-LOOK NOW."

Nani almost bounced out of her space suit. "PERMISSION REQUESTED TO-LOOK, SIR," she said, trying to keep her hands still enough to avoid reflecting the exuberant hope she was feeling.

The Captain did not respond immediately, and instead shook her hands slightly as she did when she was trying to puzzle something out. Finally she said, "QUICKEST WAY TO-SEARCH WOULD-BE TO-FIND SURFACE OF-THIS SPHERE AND LOOK IF MEDIUM ALLOWS."

Nani grinned. "I-AM GOOD AT-LOOKING." She felt the Captain laugh in response, and then felt the Captain orient herself and point. The Captain explained what she was doing with her left hand: "MY HELMET IS-POINTED UP, MY RIGHT-HAND POINTED NORTH."

Nani felt the coordinates being shown by the Captain. "AYE-AYE SIR."

"HEAD SLIGHTLY NORTH-EAST OF-STRAIGHT-UP," the Captain continued. "SWIM NO MORE THAN 30 SOL-MIN. WE CAN-TRY AGAIN LATER WHEN ALL-TOGETHER IF YOU DON'T FIND THE SURFACE."

"AYE-AYE SIR," Nani responded again.

"SEAL YOUR SUIT COMPLETELY IF YOU-NOTICE A-CHANGE IN-MEDIUM. DON'T KNOW WHAT-IS BEYOND OUR SPONGE. BE-CAREFUL-OF SURFACE MATERIAL. DON'T WANT TO-POP-IT LIKE A-SOAP-BUBBLE."

Nani agreed to all the restrictions, and then ate and drank

in preparation for leaving. The Captain oriented herself to Up and North once more, giving Nani a steady count of seconds so she could time her 30 sol-min swim. The Captain had an excellent internal clock while Nani had almost none, so Nani tried to relax, feel, and memorize the slow and steady rhythm of the seconds she was being given.

After the Captain did a final check of Nani's suit and anchored them together with a thin flexible micro-dyneem thread, she bid Nani "SAFE MISSION!" and pushed her up and northeast. Just as Nani was about to lose contact with the Captain, she felt her sign, "DO WASTE-CYCLE 15 SOL-MIN AWAY."

"NO SHIT!" responded Nani.

"EXACTLY!" said the Captain before she gave Nani a final hard boost in the right direction.

It took Nani just a couple of strokes to feel alone in the universe again. She decided on a rate of about six seconds per breath, three steady seconds in and three steady seconds out, ten breaths to a minute, 150 breaths to her waste-cycle stop. She started with a modified breast stroke. Then she switched to a faster, more efficient crawl, at all times keeping the thread that anchored her to the Captain playing out steadily, and as straight as she could. She knew from years of swimming in her home-ship pool that she pulled right slightly, so every tenth stroke she threw in an extra left stroke to keep her moving in the correct direction. If she thought about swimming and breathing, she could ignore the dark surrounding her. She stopped briefly for her waste cycle and then resumed, double-checking all the seals on her suit, and started off again.

As she reached 140 breaths, she began to worry. Nothing was changing. She was still in a dark world with no discernible features except the taut thread below her. She swam for ten more deliberately slow breaths, stilled herself, and reached out her arms, trying to feel for something, anything. She thought the goo was just a little thicker than it had been nearer the middle of the sphere, but she could be imagining that because she was tired and all motions seemed slower. She thought something might be changing but the suit dulled her sense of touch, the one sense she needed most right now.

"F-ING SPACE-BALLS," she announced to the world as she lost patience and yanked off her glove. It would either kill her or save her to be able to feel what was going on. The first thing she noticed was the shock of cold on her hand. As she twisted her right hand slowly in the goo, she felt the cold coming from the direction she had been going, perhaps from the surface of the sphere they were trapped in. She put her hand back in her glove, firmly closed the seal, and started swimming again. A couple of strokes later she began to feel the cold through the suit, the familiar cold of the vacuum, a cold she knew well. Soon her left hand banged into something, or perhaps slid into something. The texture changed from sponge to a stretchy rubbery substance. She pushed her head up until her helmet touched the new surface. She was at the membrane of the sphere. And it was translucent, almost transparent. And above her was the ordinary darkness of the vacuum with pinpoints of stars distorted by the membrane. The glorious night sky that she loved with the addition of a twin pair of dark red smudges, what had to be Luhman 16 A and B. She almost cried from relief. She could see again.

But it seemed as if she was looking through a mist at the sky. She felt the membrane and it dissolved between her fingers as she gingerly tried to pinch it. She might well be looking through membrane mist, she realized. Detaching molecules could be clouding above the surface. She drank in the sights, blurred as they were, and tried to see the contours of this world beyond the darkness of the goo. She felt for the long steady rhythm of Up. She found it easily. It felt strong up at the surface and she oriented herself towards it. In the distance, in the direction of the buzz, was an object perched on the horizon of the sphere. Was it part of what was keeping the sphere together? She had no idea. She couldn't make out the shape, just could see that it broke the smooth surface all around her. The buzz of Up was being created by it. She then felt for the dimmer sharp fast buzz of North, where the other set of waves that the Captain had marked were coming from. She couldn't see it. It would probably be well beyond the sphere horizon, but the quick rhythm let her orient herself.

She pointed herself north and then slowly started turning

herself east, trying to discern any changes, any breaks in the surface that could indicate where *The Blink* was. She tried to take in every moment of the sky, storing visions to keep her sane when she had to enter the darkness again.

Then she saw it, a blur of light at the surface towards the northeast.

She swam towards it. As she got closer, she realized it was a rainbow, light from an object below the surface of the sphere refracting through the membrane and the mists above. *The Blink* was shining her light for the universe to see and she made an f-ing glorious rainbow. Nani had never seen anything more beautiful in her life. Home was marked by a rainbow.

Cramped and cranky as *The Blink* was, Nani could live in that tin can. She could be an old-fashioned ordinary Spacer. And the rest of her crew could survive there as well. And she needed to let them know. She stilled herself, oriented herself once again to North, and then marked the rainbow as situated 40° to the east of North. She wasn't sure what the refraction index of the surface membrane and mist was, but 40° northeast was a start to the crew finding their way back home. She stared for many minutes as the colors shifted, mists moving across the surface of the sphere, and finally dove down to follow the thin thread anchoring her back to the Captain.

The 300 slow breaths and bunch of fast breaths back to the Captain seemed shorter. Her head buzzed with visions of the rainbow around *The Blink* and the object that marked Up, and concerns about what shape *The Blink* was in. Was it habitable, movable, flyable? At her 300th breath, she could feel tugs coming from the end of her thread lifeline.

The Captain was there at the end of the lifeline, as she had been when Nani started off. Nani almost bounced with excitement as she described her findings to the Captain, drawing the object at the Up pole and then the gorgeous rainbow made by what was most likely their ship.

"GOOD JOB!" signed the Captain. She seemed about to go on when she paused. Then she started again: "HANDS REPORTS BY-MORSE HE AND CREW COMING." Nani realized that the minute vibrations that she'd barely sensed were actually minute tugs on the micro-dyneem thread attached to the Captain's center. Something in Nani relaxed. Having the full contingent of the crew meant they had all the talents of everyone. They were going to get through this. A few minutes later, Gorilla, Olivia, and Janus arrived at their location. Nani hugged Olivia hello, shook hands with Janus, and got the story of their rescue. Olivia and Janus had found each other and then Gorilla had found them and brought them back to the Captain. After Gorilla and Olivia finished telling their tale (Janus was not very communicative), the Captain announced, "NANI FOUND THE-SHIP."

"YAY NANI!" cheered Olivia, and congratulations from the men quickly followed.

"GIVEN CHANCES OF-SURVIVING BETTER IN-OUR-SHIP, WE

SHOULD FIND SHIP A-S-A-P," signed the Captain. Gorilla and Olivia's responses were enthusiastic, but Janus's assent was lackluster. The Captain seemed to notice this. She asked if Eyes Nani and Hands Jacksom would be willing to go on an exploration to find the ship.

Both Nani and Gorilla immediately responded, "AYE-AYE CAPTAIN." Nani, the Captain, and Janus calculated the probable distance and angles to the ship and then Nani and Gorilla practiced maneuvering. Now that he knew what to feel for, Gorilla had a keener sense of where Up and North were, but Nani had the better sense of how to calculate the angles off the poles. They repeated Nani's previous journey up to the surface of the sphere they were in, each swimming attached to a micro-dyneem thread, Nani following in Gorilla's strong wake. The swishing ahead of her made her feel less alone in the f-ing goo. She pretended once again she was swimming in her home-ship pool with her eyes closed, just feeling the waves ahead of her, counting slowly to 300, and then swimming until she could feel the cold of the vacuum seeping past her suit. She tapped Gorilla's foot with Morse code: "S-O-O-N A-T T-O-P." A couple more strokes and their heads hit the membrane around their sphere.

"WOW," signed Gorilla as he popped his head up to the membrane and saw the expanse of space: "GORGEOUS."

"YEAH!" replied Nani with heart. She was glad somebody else was at least temporarily free of the goo. She pointed towards the Up pole, and then asked Gorilla to point to North and tried to feel for the sharp pulse of the pole. Once Gorilla pointed and oriented them, she scanned the horizon. They had come up in a slightly different place from where she had surfaced before. She had to search for her rainbow. Her heart sank as she strained her eyes to see the glow that had given her such joy before. Finally, she saw a glimmer at the horizon. She pointed Gorilla's hand in the direction of what she hoped was the ship.

"NOT SEE," signed Gorilla, but he followed her as she began to swim to the glimmer. Finally, the glimmer began to glow with the colors of the rainbow.

"NICE!" he signed at the sight. She gave a deep sigh of relief. She did have her bearings and could bring him to the ship.

They continued to swim at the surface, keeping their eyes on the glow. It took them a while until they could see any sign of the ship, and even then it was just a ripple at the surface of the goo.

"KNOW ORIENTATION?" asked Gorilla.

Nani squinted at the light and slight deformations at the surface and replied the cockpit might be near the top and oriented towards them, but that was only a guess.

"YOU STAY HERE," signed Gorilla, and then dove beneath the surface. Nani grabbed his micro-dyneem thread as he dove. She felt the thread tighten in her hands as he moved towards the vehicle. The movements she felt on the thread were smooth, evidence of Gorilla's steady strokes forward. Then she felt a sharp tug on the line and suddenly it went limp in her hands.

"SHIT!" she thought. Micro-dyneem was incredibly tough but it was possible to cut with something sharp. Her best guess was that fragments from the ship had severed the line. She was also worried that something had happened to Gorilla. She slowly moved down into the sphere of goo, once again losing her precious vision as she did. She moved her arms out in front of her to feel for any objects from the ship. She felt for signs of communication but did not sense anything. She gingerly began dolphin kicking her way to the ship. As she swam, she pushed away fragments, from pea sized to plate sized and probably hull fragments. As she got closer, she could feel waves. Morse code, perhaps? So hard to distinguish short from long strokes and where one letter ended and the next began.

"O-T-S-Y U-O-T D-S-E."

"WRONG! TRY AGAIN!" she told herself, and waited for the message to come again. When it came she realized she was screwing up the dots and dashes.

"S-T-O-Y U-S-E D-O-J-F...S-T-O-P U-S-E-D O-O-R.

"STOP, USE DOOR," she finally translated. Her heart sank. Gorilla was indicating something was wrong with the front of the ship where he had been heading. Given they had been pushed out of the ship after the white light appeared, the light or something else had cut through their hull. And cutting created fragments. Probably the same fragments that had cut his thread had been severed. "O-K," she signaled back in Morse, and his movements stilled. She was not sure he was at the bridge deck end of the ship but she started moving again, this time pointing about 60° left of where she had been headed. She felt the goo thin, making her hope that she was near her target, when she felt a sharp tug on her micro-dyneem thread and then no resistance on her line.

"SHIT! MY LINE SNAPPED SAME-AS GORILLA'S," she thought. She tried to feel for the other part of the line but she just came up with the short end. She panicked for a moment and then said, "FIND SHIP" to herself. That was why she and Gorilla had come all this distance. The ship meant life. She moved forward slowly, carefully pushing fragments out of her way, hoping to hit the ship. Her kicks were much less efficient than swimming with her full body and it felt like it took forever. She dreaded somehow missing the ship, but she kept clearing debris from her path so she knew that she must still be in range.

Finally, the goo thinned further and her hands bumped the solid surface of the ship. She let go of the breath that she hadn't realized she had been holding. She ran her hands across the ship. This part at least felt intact. She tried to recognize which part of the ship she was touching, but the smooth hull gave no information through her gloves. She cursed and tore them off. She moved her hands along the surface until she recognized the faint parallel lines that scored the helm. The door was marked by lines perpendicular to the horizontal scoring. She hugged her body to the ship and inched her way along, sweeping her hand up and down to find the slight break in the ship's hull marking the main exit hatch. At last she found it and then felt for the dimensions of the hatch, slightly broader than her arm span. She was short. The men on the crew and maybe Olivia could have reached across.

On the middle right side of the hatch, she found the security pad but it didn't read her handprint or glove print. She was able to manually enter the security code B-R-I-D-G-M-A-N-1-8-2-9, fairly obvious if you knew the Captain but obscure to most, and the hatch started to fall forward into the goo. Nani reached up and pried the door open enough to tumble into the ship. She took off her helmet and looked around, profoundly relieved to be able to see the familiar contours of the ship lit by strangely bright emergency lights. She remembered them in the past seeming to be very dim. The airlock seemed intact and she was able to get through it and into the crew lounge, which was also intact. As she moved towards the bridge, though, she could see more damage to the interior. She also began to worry because she felt no movement from Gorilla.

She rarely used her voice. She had a Deaf voice and never had any interest in making it sound less Deaf, but she called out in case Gorilla could hear her. "Gaaaarr," she called but could feel no movement in response. Just beyond the crew quarters, the bridge deck was smashed to pieces and floating in goo. It looked jaggedly sliced off from the rest of the ship. She attached herself to the crew quarters with a strong safety line, donned her helmet and gloves for protection, and gingerly went out into what had been the bridge. Feeling her way through the right side of the goo, she felt the round top of a helmet but got no response when she knocked on the hard surface. She didn't usually pray to any god or spirit but she sent pleas of "NOT DEAD, NOT DEAD" into the universe as she pulled Gorilla's unresponsive body through the crew cabin hatch and back into the main part of the ship.

Once in the light again, she saw that a large hull fragment had pierced his left side and that blood was seeping out from the wound. She carefully took off his helmet and breathed a deep sigh of relief when she felt a light pulse at his throat, but his skin was cold and clammy and he was still unresponsive. She stretched him out in the galley way and went to find the emergency first aid box. The med station would have been better, but it was on the other side of the ship and didn't function well on emergency power. She found the box, thankfully undamaged, and made her way back to the corridor.

She got the kit ready and started. She began by lightly spraying his face with water and wiping it down. He flinched slightly but did not wake. She then set to clipping off his suit around the wound, careful to save the pieces so they could repair it later. They were too far from home to waste suit mats. She readied her cleaning solutions, wound glue, gauze, and bandaging materials and then removed the debris slice with a sharp pull. Blood seeped but did not gush. She quickly washed the area, glued the jagged wound together as best she could, and then bound it all with gauze and a tight bandage wrapped with some difficulty all around his lower chest.

He opened his mouth and she could feel his vocal cords moving in what was probably a groan of pain. His breathing was slow and shallow but steady, so she felt willing to risk giving him a bit of pain medication. He was going to be unhappy. But living and unhappy was far better than dead. She tidied him and the corridor the best she could, wrote a note saying, "Gone for the rest of the crew, back soon," and got ready to leave. She hated leaving the relative familiarity of the ship. Even damaged, *The Blink* was infinitely more comfortable than the darkness of the goo, but Gorilla would probably die without the formal medical help Olivia could offer, and the crew needed the modest shelter *The Blink* could offer.

Given that micro-dyneem snapped in the debris field, she found a large reel of safety cord to bring with her as an anchor to the ship and as a guide for the rest of the crew to find their way back. She attached one end of the reel to an exterior pop tab next to the main hatch, and the other end to her midpoint tool belt, and squeezed her way out of the partially opened hatch and into the hated goo again. She swam until she was free of the debris field and then a little further for safety, and finally allowed herself to head for the surface again. With every stroke, she hoped her hand would find one of the two micro-dyneem threads they'd lost, but she found nothing but ship debris. She would just have to navigate by eye and feel.

The steady pulse of Up was easy to feel once she surfaced, but the sharp pulses of North were harder to detect. She had to take her gloves off again until she could finally feel its presence. She began a slow swim along the surface towards Up. Her parents, her real Chilmark parents, used to joke that she was a ball of fast-twitch muscles. She wished she had some more slow-twitch muscles at this point. She felt exhausted. Getting to *The Blink* and caring for Gorilla had taken everything from her. But she had to make it back to the others. They needed her. And Jacksom needed Olivia and the crew.

She halted, wanting to stop and just sleep forever under the blurry stars, but she forced herself to start again. She found a rhythm that was smooth but just a little painful. She concentrated on the sharpness of the pain to keep herself awake and moving. Eventually, when she looked up to check her course, she could see the dim outline of Up and the faded rainbow of the ship in the distance. She felt for Up and North and they seemed to be the right strength for her dive point. She stared at the line between Up and the ship, and it looked as she remembered it. It was her best guess for the dive point.

She closed her eyes for a second and then jerked herself

awake a few seconds, a minute, perhaps longer than that, later. She still felt exhausted. But she hydrated, took nutrition, checked her coordinates one more time, and dove into the goo again, trying to breathe in and out at her steady six-second breathing pace. It didn't work well. She was so tired that she couldn't concentrate on her breaths. Instead she just told herself to swim 300 strokes. One to 50 were painful. For 50 to 100, she fell into a rhythm that began to put her to sleep. At 100, she tried to feel for Up and North and to reorient herself, visualizing where she was and where she needed to go. At 150, she took off her gloves, just to feel something because not being able to see was driving her mad. The sensation of the goo foam on her hands gave her something to think about. She sensed movements but couldn't figure out where they were coming from. She kept swimming, trying to keep going down. She didn't know how many strokes she'd done. Had no idea of her breaths. She was not made for darkness. It was beginning to eat her. To swallow and digest her…

She awoke with a start and thrashed. "JUST GOO," she told herself, "JUST GOO." She went back to swimming for a while and then stopped to feel. Some rhythm was there, a rolling human rhythm. Maybe more than one rhythm. Yes. She swam a little further. There was rhythm.

And then her hand touched something. A part of a suit. A second later the Captain's hand was in her hand, signing, "PAH, GOOD JOB, NANI. PAH!"

Olivia was hugging her and patting her. She even got a pat from what felt like Janus. Then explanations, kept as brief as possible, began. Jacksom was hurt and needed Olivia's medical skills. The bridge was destroyed but the rest of the ship seemed intact. Nani was attached to the ship by a reel of space line but she had no idea where the reel was. She had been too exhausted to keep track of it. Perhaps it was back at the surface. The micro threads had been snapped by debris.

As she was explaining this to the Captain and Olivia, she could feel them starting to move up, reversing the direction in which she had been swimming.

The Captain explained that she would be the lead in heading back up the safety line. She ordered Janus to assist Nani, and Olivia to help Janus when necessary. Together, they made their way back up to the surface, Nani letting herself be pulled most of the time by Janus. It wasn't a gentle pull, more of an insistent yank, but it kept her going. Every once in a while, she felt an encouraging pat from Olivia. Soon they reached the cold edges of the sphere and then the transparent film. Nani felt for the rhythms of Up and North and then once again saw a dim rainbow glow from the ship. Her safety line seemed to be intact, and they made their way along the surface and then dived down through the debris to the hatch of the ship, tumbling out of the goo into the air lock. They closed the hatch and then the inner hatch opened. Gorilla stood there, looking awful but alive.

THE DARKNESS OF GOO

"Pah, welcome home!" he signed to all of them. She had made it. They had made it. They were safe. As safe as they could be in this sphere of goo years away from the nearest known settled planet. So many questions, so much to explore, so much they needed to know. But for now, she no longer had to thrash her way through the goo. Through life. She closed her eyes and let the darkness of unconsciousness come to her.

The Reject

by Timothy Lamoureux

BLAZING THROUGH SPACE, Rick Truss, the captain of the *Morlaix*, along with first officer Kyle O'Brian and tactical officer Pete Goff, watched the clock, waiting for the fourth member of their crew. The jangling of his belt echoed down the corridors from the restroom near the mess hall before he burst onto the bridge, his face flushed. Captain Truss looked up from the digital time display. "You're late again, Ronan."

Ronan Lecrom, the ship's chief engineer and executive chef (as he'd tell you), lurched into his seat at the engineering terminal and responded, "Sorry, Rick. I've been having a flare-up this week."

Pete pitched in, "You'd think in the year 2234 they'd have cured that by now." He stretched, standing and lifting his leg over the back of his chair.

Ronan sighed. "Sadly, Pete, I don't have anything people care about, like erectile dysfunction."

Kyle chuckled. "Well, it's a good thing they cured that one for where we're going." His friends stared at him while the engine hummed. "I mean, you know, for other people obviously. Not us. We're young and athletic… um, let's chart this course, Captain?"

Captain Truss had faith in the little ship, the *Morlaix*. The purloined surgical strike ship made up for its limited armaments with speed. The Terran Empire would like it back, but Truss and the crew needed it for their operations. After years of operation and few materials for maintenance, it persisted as a patchwork of either alien or antique parts and jury-rigged repairs. They loved their sleek interstellar smuggling machine.

Captain Truss pulled up the holographic star chart. "To make a little extra scratch on the way to drop off our shipment of all those lovely goods we smuggled off Zeta-10, we're swinging around the Tau Ceti system…." The display mapped the course as he plugged numbers. He continued after entering the rest of the coordinates, "Leading us to the Yitton Sperm Bank, which apparently has a paucity of human DNA, meaning big profits for us. The beauty of it is, if we blast through the asteroid field ten light-years away, we arrive to our buyers right… here." The star chart zoomed into the earthlike planet. "To Kepler and its oppressed freedom fighters with large quantities of rhodium, the thinking man's platinum."

Using his own display, Kyle added, "And the latest scans show no interstellar delays on your mapped route, sir."

Ronan gave a thumbs-up, reading the engine's diagnostics.

"We can easily maintain the speed you've set, Rick. Our engine is functioning in normal parameters."

Chuckling, Rick said, "Well then, just stay alert. We're on the outskirts of the known galaxy, nobody really knows what's past that place. Sounds like we'll make our run though, unless we get delayed due to stage fright at YSB."

Pete smirked, "Let's hope they have quality holograms."

Kyle laughed. "That would be important." The *Morlaix* adjusted course to YSB.

AS THE HOURS dragged on with no news, each crew member remained at his post with a chosen distraction. Ronan closely examined a treatise on increasing the efficiency of plasma weapons. Shorter than the rest of the crew, he hunched over his desk and display, a large clear screen in a Spartan steel workstation. In his rush to the bridge this morning he had failed to clean his glasses, and smudges made it hard to see. He ran his fingers through his shock of black hair, entranced by the destructive power he could add to his own arsenal with a few minor tweaks.

Pete had his earphones in and was putting together a mix, pursuing his dream of being a space DJ.

Kyle had his fantasy sports models underway, and he crunched numbers to determine if he wanted the so-called Space Ruth on his team.

Rick continued a long-standing challenge against the ship's computer for a high score in Galactus. His love of video games belied the love of athletics which he shared with his crewmates. He'd first met Kyle wrestling in college, and Pete was a star track athlete. Rick had no metrics to evaluate just how much their genetics would be worth to the Yittons. Would his brown eyes and chestnut hair increase the value of his DNA? He had to assume that overall they'd be high value because every member of the crew had met at Lemaitre University, the so-called Ivy of Mars. Intelligence, good genes, good looks, health, and height made a valuable combination.

Yitton would have no record of their dishonorable discharge from the military after Ronan lied about having Crohn's Disease and the brass ejected all of them for covering for him. Even after years of service, and a rare period of reliable health, the fact that his pals sneaked him medication to control the illness had evoked merciless retribution from the top brass. Rick thanked the stars every day that he had managed to commandeer a ship after that in order to get their business venture off the ground.

Ronan's timer distracted everyone from their distractions. Cheerfully he said, "Alright guys, time for lunch, I'll cook it up."

Kyle groaned. "Not more of those kale salad, no-carbs, no-sugar, no-nothing tasteless abominations you call lunch."

Ronan showed all his teeth. "Just the same! The perfect

diet to get me out of this funk. Besides, a low-fat, low-sugar diet improves sperm quality, supposedly even taste, and that can only help us when we reach the Yittons tomorrow night."

Kyle snapped back, "How's that going to matter? It's not like they're gonna eat it."

Ronan jutted his jaw to the side, considering. "How do you know? It's not like anyone knows much about these Yittons. This could be a buffet. Maybe this is how they get their condiments."

Pete removed his headphones. "Just as long as it's not where you get yours, I don't care." Punching Kyle on the shoulder as he headed toward the mess, he added, "I like healthy eating."

As they got up to leave Rick interjected, "I had to stay on the bridge yesterday. Kyle, you stay here while we eat and take the second lunch shift."

Kyle managed to return to his seat without grumbling. "Aye, sir."

Rick slapped Ronan on the back. "You know what though, seriously, I'd love a nice shepherd's pie one of these days. When's the last time we had something like that?"

Flinching, Ronan responded, "We're out of potatoes."

While forcing himself to chew the mountain of insubstantial greens before him, Rick had one thought running through his mind: *I'm so glad we're making some extra cash soon at that sperm bank.* He dreamed of pillowy mounds of mashed potatoes drenched in gravy, with hearty beef and carrots piled high underneath a flaky and crispy pie crust.

"Sir, THE SPACE station is coming up on the scanner. With our approach vector we'll arrive in the next four hours," Pete announced.

"Hail them and request docking instructions. Let them know we're here to make a deposit," said Rick.

Pete hailed them on audio only, as was his preference. He always said letting people know the *Morlaix* was a rickety bucket, with a steel bridge comprised of spare parts and hope and with only a four-man crew, hurt the team tactically.

A voice crackled as Kyle adjusted the gain. "*Morlaix*, welcome to the Yitton Tau Ceti Reproductive Health Center. Docking Bay four will be ready for you upon your estimated arrival. We look forward to you serving us."

Pete responded, "Roger." He turned to the other men on the bridge. "We're serving them? Must be a translation error."

"It's not called the Sperm Bank?" Ronan scoffed.

Rick sighed. "They do other things. It's too bad none of you guys have ovaries—selling eggs is the jackpot."

Turning back to his view screen, Rick ordered his tactical officer, "The moment we get into visual range, I want that gonad bank on the viewer. Everyone, look alert. This is the first time we've been here. Who even knows what other ships will be around?" Glancing at Ronan he added, "We might see some old friends from the academy days."

"We're low on ammo," Kyle lamented.

Rick paused before waving his hand. "Better hope we don't get jacked before we… Well, look alive, everyone."

They sat in nervous silence while the engine hummed. As time dragged on, they felt the weight of anticipation as they listened for the scanner's proximity alarm to inform them of certain death from some sort of hunter-class or warship. The longer they waited the more certain it became.

Eventually, though, Pete broke the silence: "We have a visual!" Everyone exhaled.

"What are you waiting for? Get it up, officer," Kyle said.

Ronan chuckled. "Do you really not say stuff like this on purpose? We should write your quotes down on the board in the rec room."

"Oh yeah? Why not write yours in the bathroom?" Kyle said without looking up.

"That's cold, man," Ronan answered in monotone, entranced by the main viewer's loading screen.

Pete put the station on screen.

They noticed the Reproductive Center's dozens of neutron torpedo ports and various blast arrays, its defenses stacked layer upon layer. Pete whistled, "For a small space station, they know to pack efficiently for protection."

Rick scoffed. "I wonder if they have all those weapons to

protect themselves from us and our sector, or if there's something out past the Yittons, in uncharted space, that we don't want to meet."

Ronan replied, "Uncharted space still freaks me out."

Kyle added, "Doesn't matter—we won't be here long, and being on that space station could be the safest we've been since Mars."

"Safe?" Pete said. "Where's your sense of adventure?"

"You're right," Kyle conceded. "I can't wait to check this place out."

Ronan chuckled. "Just don't get too excited."

Kyle laughed. "What? I thought I was the one who kept saying stuff like that by accident."

Ronan looked at him, grinning. "Well, sure, but when I say it, it's on purpose."

The captain snapped, "Quiet down, morons, we're only approaching an unknown space station in an unknown part of space manned by an unknown species. Pete, check the manifest. Can we bring weapons onboard?"

Pete answered, "I'm checking, but I doubt it."

Rick rolled his eyes. "Just check anyway, please."

Pete reread his screen. "Yeah, when you check their docking instructions it specifies you must leave all weapons behind, but..." he finished sarcastically, "they guarantee your safety." He held up his hands in dismay. "Haven't these guys ever read the 45th Amendment?"

The captain nodded but said, "The smart smugglers only smuggle when there's profit in it. I can't imagine this is some sort of weird kill trap, especially not for our junker rig. They could have turned us away."

"Junker rig?" Ronan stood up.

"What, you're too offended to remain seated?" scoffed the captain.

"No, I need to use the toilet before we get there," Ronan said as he got up.

"We might need you! We're docking in an hour and we're approaching them quickly!" Rick snapped.

"That's why I'm doing it now! This is my window, Cap'n," rejoined Ronan.

"All right. Fine, Ronan." Rick waved his hand. "Everyone else, get ready."

THE LITTLE SHIP slowed and floated toward Docking Bay 4. Ronan rejoined his friends on the bridge in time to see the porthole open up, forming a metallic maw beyond which eerie, pale lights highlighted the tractor beam that dragged them in after they powered down the engine. "OK guys, stash the weapons," Kyle ordered as he removed hidden weapons from his boot holsters and underneath his trench coat, locking them into the bridge's armory. Ronan, Pete, and Rick followed suit.

"I really hate being without a firearm," Pete moaned.

Ronan nodded. "It's like part of my body. Nobody ever asks you to take your teeth out. Maybe they should be afraid I'd bite them."

Kyle laughed. "They should be worried about your other end. Thanks for joining us in the nick of time."

Ronan unholstered his sidearm. "And miss all of this? The great unknown?"

The ship lurched to a halt. "We must be docked. Everyone get to the airlock. Let's not keep them waiting," ordered the captain.

The docking bay had high steel beams, a massive ceiling that could dock a ship six times the size of the *Morlaix*, and was fully automated. Lights formed an arrow in the floor, pointing toward a nearby portcullis. "Well, I guess that cuts down on translation," observed Ronan. "Universal symbol for *walk this way*." Everyone else remained silent.

The captain led the way. After crossing through the large portal, which rumbled open as they approached, they entered a long, fluorescently lit corridor with white tiled floors and a beige ceiling. Smaller, human-sized white doors lined the halls, with little bronze knobs on each of them. A rectangular sign with a picture of a reception desk, complete with a reception-ist, hung from the ceiling fifteen feet in front of them, with an arrow pointing upward. They shared a look that said, "Let's continue on, I suppose."

Ronan added, "Guys, try to figure out what sign is for the

restrooms, specifically the men's room. They have no reason to follow usual conventions—I mean, for all we know the species running this bank has a triangular lower body."

"I wouldn't mind peeing right about now myself," Kyle agreed.

At the end of the hallway, after walking a brisk minute, they found a heavy door painted light blue with the signature bronze knob. "That's a nice change of pace from the white," noted Kyle. His voice echoed in the hall. Rick reached out, twisted the knob, and creaked the door open. They couldn't believe their eyes.

"GREAT. AN INTERGALACTIC waiting room, just like I've always dreamed of," Ronan muttered while absentmindedly leafing through a magazine.

Rick wondered where the magazines came from. The receptionist, seated behind the counter and obscured by fogged glass, seemingly read his mind and answered, "We prepare the waiting room with items to put our patrons at ease. I trust these magazines will make you feel at home."

Ronan exclaimed, "Hey, check it out! *National Geographic* explains how the ancient Egyptians used to mummify people."

Kyle picked up another magazine. "Marilyn Monroe?" He nudged the captain. "I guess it makes sense given where we are, huh?"

Rick responded drily, "We're in a lobby. It's a little anti-quated, but as long as they pay I don't really care."

The sperm bank even had the long waits of any doctor's office on Earth. Sitting in stiff, cloth-softened chairs with metal legs, the crew observed the banal surroundings. They stared at beige walls with nonrepresentational art in bland primary colors lacking any real complexity. Stacks of old magazines and newspapers lay on top of small, round glass coffee tables that bookended the rows of grayish-purple chairs. "Vivid" described nothing in the place. Drained of energy by the ennui permeating the bland room, the captain realized he'd forgotten to check in.

He walked up to the fogged glass, and the receptionist's form behind the glass appeared fairly human. She had no extra hands or anything else, but he could only see a silhouette. At most, he could tell her skin had approximately the same tone as her uniform. "So do we need to check in?" he asked. She responded curtly, her voice flat and emotionless, that he needed to fill out some forms but they were already checked in.

As he walked away with four clipboards and four forms to bring to his friends, it occurred to him that her voice had the quality of a 1920's radio broadcast. He shook off that bizarre notion and handed the forms out to his friends.

Ronan guffawed, "The only thing better than an intergalactic waiting room is intergalactic paperwork." He paused and added as an afterthought, "This whole place is so strange. It's like an Earth diorama and we're in it."

Kyle responded, "They said they plan ahead. Plus, I've never been to an alien waiting room. If everyone's humanoid I don't see why it'd be any different."

"Sure, but it's all pretty out of place. Like if someone recreated things from Earth from third-hand accounts," Pete added.

The captain agreed, "It's all very weird, for numerous reasons. Why would they want human sperm, for example? But they pay." He looked up from his paperwork. "We get in. We get paid. We get out. That's it."

They read through the forms and began filling out the usual: name, place of birth, and then more specific questions like IQ, height, whether they had any genetic disorders—all questions geared at measuring their level of fitness and the value contained in their genetic code.

"Do we lie about our height and weight on these?" Kyle nudged Ronan. "Just asking for a friend."

The captain sighed. "No chances, man."

Kyle guffawed. "Six four, green eyes, handsome, two hundred thirty pounds of pure muscle. Come on, ladies!"

Pete joined in, "Blond hair, blue eyes, six two, two twenty, ladies!"

Rick rolled his eyes. "Six two, chestnut hair, like a horse. Ride on, ladies!"

Shuffling in his seat, Ronan said, "Guys, I'm worried about

this form. It asks whether I have any illnesses."

Rick said, "Just go up and ask. We're not lying for you about this again."

Ronan demurred, "You think?"

"It worked out so well last time," the captain said flatly.

Ronan continued, "But they aren't going to track us down later. They'd have to check right away…." He trailed off, as the captain just looked at him, his lips tight.

"Fine." Ronan approached the glass in defeat and asked, "Would Crohn's disqualify someone from donating any sperm here?"

The shape behind the glass stated in her tinny voice, "Yes, it is a genetic disorder. I'm afraid you will have to wait back here when we let your friends in."

Crestfallen, Ronan had to ask, "Well, do you at least have a bathroom back there I can use?"

She buzzed open a door to the left of the counter. "Take a right and use the third door on your left."

He stepped into a wide hallway, with more of the same nondescript tiles and walls. The hallway, however, was enormous. It disappeared out into a vanishing point like an old Renaissance painting, and Ronan felt a little dizzy staring out at it. Still, he turned and went down the intersecting hallway to the right. The first two doors lacked any markings, but the last had a sperm-shaped decal. *Thematically appropriate, and I guess no race around the galaxy will get confused,*

Ronan said to himself. He turned the cold bronze knob, far colder than the ambient, unnoticeable temperature of the rest of the station, and opened the door.

The bathroom was extremely large, outfitted with numerous stalls, with sonic sinks, dryers, and even, as he looked in, bidets in some of the stalls. He instinctively checked under them because he hated taking care of business with anyone else around. To his relief, he found himself alone.

He entered the furthest stall and prepared himself, finally able to think without any distractions. Despite the pain in his bowels, he appreciated these moments of privacy. It's never enjoyable to be told you're not fit to procreate. *What do they know though? Them, the military, they're always so preoccupied with what you can't do, they never think of all the things you have in your favor.* Ronan began to feel better, sitting there in that stall. He was a valuable member of a ragtag crew of spacemen who followed their own rules, made their own way, and forged their own destiny.

But they get to make extra money donating genetic material for the sperm bank.

"Even aliens are jerks," Ronan muttered. His voice echoed in the empty restroom. He began to wonder how long he had been sitting there, and started to become self-conscious. "Come on, everybody likes the solitude. Nobody's timing you," he told himself.

He knew they were all timing him.

Reluctantly, Ronan got up, cleaned himself with a sonic cleanser and the bidet, and washed his hands. He dried his hands on his duster, as he never had anything better to use on the *Morlaix*.

Stepping out of the bathroom, he ran into his three friends in the hallway. They all pointed to their wrists, jokingly.

"We're up," Rick said. "Just wait for us, we'll be back soon."

"Some sooner than others," Pete laughed while nudging Kyle.

Ronan bid them good luck and watched them walk down the impossibly long hallway, their forms getting smaller and smaller as they continued. He wanted to yell at them to ask how far down they were going, but he thought better of it and returned to the waiting room.

He sat in silence in the uncomfortable chair until he lost track of time. He half-dozed, unable to banish thoughts invading his head about their shared time back on Mars in the military. They had all, Ronan included, been destined to become first class officers. The Terran Empire was going to shower them with success, but plans change unexpectedly. He wondered if "To a Mouse" was in one of those magazines and that's why he was stuck on this idea. They'd probably all have found wives and had children by now if they'd never gotten kicked off the beaten path. Kicked off. He mulled over that in his mind. *What did I do wrong?* The old question resurfaced.

The unsatisfying answer resurrected itself. *I wanted to do something they told me I couldn't because of something I never had control over.*

He heard the rest of the crew return. They stiffly walked out of the hallway and thanked the receptionist, and Rick waved for Ronan to follow. Ronan shook himself and got up, hurrying to catch up with them. "How was it?" he asked, breathlessly.

Rick responded, "No problems. Let's return to the ship. We have work to do."

Ronan wondered what exactly the process was in there, but felt too awkward to ask. His three friends seemed quiet. Ronan piped up, "So, what's the rush? My understanding is we're actually a little ahead of schedule to make our next rendez-vous."

The captain responded, "I'm the judge of that." Ronan kept his mouth shut, along with everyone else, until they arrived at the ship.

Rick said, "No time wasting. Peter, clear us for departure, and you set the course, Kyle." Pete and Kyle responded, "Aye, Captain."

"I'll make sure that the engine is ready," Ronan said. There was no reply. "OK...." he muttered to nobody.

"We're clear, let's go," the captain ordered Kyle. And the *Morlaix* floated out into space and blasted away from the Sperm Bank.

THREE DAYS AFTER leaving the station, Ronan had barely said a word to anyone else on board. He thought twice before opening his mouth. He analyzed what the reaction would be. His crewmates didn't start conversations, and nobody laughed; they sat silently at their posts on the bridge. Ronan lollygagged in the exercise room and pondered excuses to spend extra time with the engine. He'd already run a diagnostic every day. Munchausen's by engine gave him an empty feeling in his stomach—and, somehow, simultaneously additional pressure in his gut.

Kyle walked in wordlessly and began to curl with sixty-pound dumbbells. He breathed through his nose, eyes forward. As Ronan finished his 200-pound bench, his voice caught in his throat, and he couldn't hear anything but the blood pounding in his ears. He uttered incomprehensible syllables under his breath that garnered the same reaction from Kyle as anything in the past three days. He headed out to the engine room.

The ship had small corridors with dim, flickering lights. Brighter lights cost money. A small, two-deck ship, it housed the engine in the lower deck amid a series of catwalks and tubing corridors jury-rigged to power the ship far more efficiently than the antiquated technology would otherwise suggest. Ronan felt a piece of himself was reflected in this ship;

the rusted hull hid those sparky power couplings and the circuitry that represented his own insides. Someone else designed and built this ship, but the ship grew up into his image. Ronan walked past the airlock, then past the living quarters, then to the catwalk by the stairs down to the engine room.

He decided to make work by examining the power supply to the bridge, so after entering the engine room he crawled into the tubing. Times like this, being any taller would have slowed him down. He barely had room for his shoulders in the tight space.

BEEP BEEP BEEP

His pill timer screamed and he jumped, slamming his head into the panel above him. Lying down, he rubbed his head and paused before pulling out his pills. He forced them down without water because he'd forgotten to bring his bottle. The pills scraped his throat all the way down. He crawled onward to the panel directly underneath the bridge. Sweating and sore, he rasped out a few breaths before deciding that he may as well nap here since he was manufacturing this work anyway. If someone asked, he was down here.

As soon as he put his head down on the metal floor, he heard the unusual sound of a power surge and felt the ship lurch. He crawled backwards towards the engine and analyzed the display. Power output had doubled.

Ronan rushed up the stairs and ran down the corridor to

the bridge. His engineer's boots clanked hard against the metal grating. His side ached. After a full workout, he struggled to run. But he ran. He burst onto the bridge. He choked out a yell. "What is going on here?"

Rick looked at him, checked the diagnostic readout near his chair, and looked back. "We're adjusting our course."

"What?" Ronan didn't understand. "What do you mean? What about our shipment to Kepler?"

The captain responded, "They can wait."

The engineer rejoined, "No, they can't. That's pretty much the whole reason they pay so well."

Rick hissed, "I'm the captain on this ship."

Ronan gathered himself. "Where are we going?"

"The planet doesn't have a name. It's past Tau Ceti." The captain pointed to a star chart. "Here."

Ronan scratched a nonexistent itch and looked at the stone-faced captain. "That's incredibly far off our route. We will never make our delivery. It's also so far, no way we'll get any more potatoes."

"I don't care," the captain said.

Ronan's eyes narrowed. "Don't care? Do you care we'll be eating nothing but MREs for half the trip? I suspect we'll run out by the time we get back."

The crew stared at him silently and the captain showed no reaction. "We'll scrounge up food along the way."

Ronan's eyebrows flattened. Gnawing his lip, he side-eyed

the captain. "What? Alien food? I can't eat alien food. As far as I know NOBODY can eat alien food. We'll starve."

"The decision is final. Check the engine and make sure we can maintain this speed until arrival. I want to be there within the month." The captain turned away.

Ronan slapped his hands together as he over-enunciated each word in response. "Wake up! Don't you hear what I am saying? We will not survive the trip. Who cares whether the engine will? A bunch of corpses hurtling through space don't enjoy it more than a bunch of corpses on a derelict ship floating around aimlessly." He paused as it occurred to him, "Though I'd rather be a corpse that got blown up—at least that's something to tell people in the afterlife."

Pete rose up from his chair and the captain ordered, "Peter, remove Ronan to the engine room and make sure he does his job. If not, persuade him."

A wave of thoughts flushed through Ronan's mind, but only one repeated: *Override controls in the engine room.* Ronan slipped out of the back and sprinted down the hallway. Cold sweat dripped to his eyebrows and he heard three men's footfalls clanging behind him. He jumped into the corridor to the engine room and slid down the railing to go downstairs. The clanging grew louder. He fiddled with the controls to lock them out of the engine room and drop the bulkhead. The clanging was almost here. He saw the three men running, their expressions blank. Ronan stopped breathing as if he were dunked in ice water.

"Come on!" Ronan breathed. The security lockout wouldn't work—it only beeped in protest. He pounded on it, but in seconds they'd be on him. He hurled himself around into the ship's tunnel system. One of the men, he didn't know who, grabbed one of his boots, but it slipped off as he wormed his way further into the ship.

He would have a speed advantage in here, but not for long. He heard two sets of footfalls bang their way up the stairs, but a third shuffled into the tube. Every breath burned, his body ached, and he could only feel pain and numbness shooting down his shoulders, but he pulled himself up a small ladder to the first floor tunnel. He slid out with a thud and crawled to hide in the nearest room, catching his breath and struggling to force life into his muscles.

He leaned back against the wall when the captain walked through the doorway. Rick barked to the other two men to stop searching and get in here. Ronan rasped, "You're not my friends, are you?"

"What gave it away?" the captain asked.

Ronan's every breath pushed needles into his throat. "The fact you didn't care about the ship's well-being, but I had suspicions before that. The quietness, the lack of passive aggression about my getting us dishonorably discharged, your apathy about potatoes."

The captain-creature motioned to Kyle's and Pete's doppelgängers. To Ronan he said, "I don't need you alive, but I'd prefer that you man your post."

Ronan lolled his head around, recognizing the room he was in. He hunched his shoulders and started to get up. "Just do one thing," he said.

The captain asked, "What?"

"Remember to exhale." Ronan burst forward, past the two men hulking over him and then past the captain-creature, launching himself and rolling. As he landed, the captain-creature reached out and grabbed his other boot, which slipped off in his hand. In his socks, the only true human on board bounced up and threw out an elbow without needing to look back. He made it through the door of the airlock before it slammed shut. "I don't know where you guys are from, but humans never make that mistake."

The captain-creature, eyes wide behind the glass, implored, "We're clones! We're human! We're your friends! You won't kill us. You can't!"

Ronan silently activated the countdown. The ship's robotic voice started, "Ten, nine, eight."

The captain screamed again, "You can't do this!"

The ship counted. "Three, two, one."

Ronan leaned against the wall across from the airlock's glass porthole, unable to look away. "I already did."

His three friends, *doppelgängers* he reminded himself, exploded out into blackness the instant the door opened.

Steam rose off their bodies and blood floated out of their mouths.

Ronan turned away. "They forgot to exhale." His knee stabbed him with every step, but Ronan took himself to the showers and some well-earned time in the restroom. Then it occurred to him: the ship was still off-course.

Dripping while running naked down the hallway, Ronan figured modesty mattered for little on an empty ship. His feet slapped the icy metal, but he ignored the discomfort and focused on the sound of his feet echoing down the corridors. When he skidded into the bridge, he halted the engines at the captain's terminal. Forgetting the impropriety, he sat in the captain's chair and began typing in the Yitton Sperm Bank's coordinates. His knee throbbed. He'd never understood why an autoimmune disorder where his own white blood cells attacked his guts would also commonly cause joint pain, but he shook it off. He avoided looking at the calculation as long as he could. Almost eight unbearable days to return to YSB. He shivered and pain shot through his knee. He sighed, "I'm naked in the captain's chair." He did not move.

Ronan closed his eyes and leaned back. He spoke to break the eerie silence on the bridge, but the words faded into dead space. "I need to get the tranquilizers. If I'm not training, eating, or getting the engines ready, I need to sleep and get my energy. I don't want to have a bathroom emergency in the middle of a gunfight."

THE ALARM PESTERED Ronan on the toilet. He hurried to his locker. "Time to trade out the engineer's boots for the combat boots." He thought about his friends' bodies and his boots floating in space. He pulled out his dark brown duster jacket, his auburn muscle shirt, and heavy-duty cargo pants. He paused a moment and hurried to the armory. The combat boots, though tight, felt right on his feet.

At the armory he strapped holsters onto nearly every part of his body. On both ankles, he attached miniature plasma blasters. He squeezed into a vest with multiple hypersonic grenades. He strapped on four holsters for laser pistols, multiple carbon-fibered laser-forged knives, and numerous additional power cells. His buckles and holsters clicked and snapped as he strapped more pistols onto his thighs, hid knives on his biceps, and strapped one more onto his chest just below his collarbone. Medikit attached to thigh. He took one high-yield laser rifle and walked to his bedroom to retrieve his pet project, the supposedly near-infinite-power, untested, and experimental cell plasma rifle. He lifted both weapons and placed them down on his bed as he packed a few more vital items: three extra pairs of underwear and an extra pair of socks.

He rushed out to survey the ship's readiness. He shuffled around the bridge, pacing while his stomach tightened and his mind invented hundreds of nightmarish outcomes for his rescue mission. Maybe they'd already killed his friends. Maybe they'd turned them into mulch. Maybe they'd eaten them. Maybe they'd decapitated them and frozen their heads in a twisted limbo of a science experiment. His stomach cramped and he had to take a moment in the bathroom. Sadly, nobody would count down how long he remained in there. He sighed and shook his head.

Ronan knew he would soon enter communications range, and he needed to put the plan in motion. Strapping his weaponry on, he got up off the toilet and walked to the bridge. He thought through his plan one more time, and imagined a thousand ways it could go wrong.

He waited.

The comm system crackled to life as the calm woman's voice that had greeted them before asked, "Why are you returning?"

Ronan pressed *Play* and his doctored recording responded in Rick's voice, "We encountered a problem and require repairs. Please allow us reentry."

He sat holding his breath as the crackling of the comm droned on.

After a time, he let out a sigh of relief when he received a response: "Acceptable. Dock in Loading Bay 4."

Ronan loaded in the coordinates. He had several hours before the ship would dock. He sat with his guns in his lap, meditating and preparing as he continued to disassemble and reassemble his weapons.

Oblivious to the passage of time, he listened to the thrusters soften to a hum on approach. The craft slowly entered into the same dock he'd landed in with his friends. He wondered if they would ever ride together again.

The ship lurched to a halt. He supposed he would soon learn the answers to all of his questions, the ones that mattered anyway. With all of his weapons strapped on and his rifles slung across his back, he got up.

He opened the airlock and marched down the hall. Visions of the floating corpses of the clones of his friends danced in his head in silent ballet. Then he stepped out of the airlock. An emaciated man, probably a clone, stood there asking about the repairs he needed. His mouth dry, Ronan responded there was some issue with the injector coils, but he didn't know tech stuff.

Relieved to have avoided discovery, Ronan stepped past the emaciated man, who asked, "But why are you so heavily armed?"

Ronan thought about that for a moment and then slammed the butt of one of his rifles into the man's face. The man stayed down. Ronan muttered to himself, pulling the pin from a thermite grenade, "I guess there's infiltration and then there's going in hot." He shrugged while counting down the charge. "It's not like they wouldn't find out." He tossed the grenade.

The explosion seared white hot, and he turned away. When he looked back, the door was a puddle on the floor, and the bland white hallway had shrapnel and black scorch marks streaking across its bland beige walls. The door across the hall screeched open, and a dozen clones armed with laser and plasma weapons poured out. Two of them looked like Rick and one of them looked like Kyle, he noted before he opened fire. In a moment of clarity, in between bursts of plasma fire, Ronan noted they all appeared imperfect—perhaps their creators hadn't finished them quite yet.

As the clones fought through the bottleneck of the door, Ronan had an easy time picking targets who couldn't shoot over one another. One shot of his modified plasma rifle seared through five targets, leaving nothing more than biological waste on the floor. He kept firing. A laser scorched past his left ear, singeing his hair. He fired back, not allowing any of them to enter past the door. He advanced toward the door, never ceasing to fire. He no longer even identified the faces of his attackers. He only saw his muzzle flash.

He felt good until the doors along the walls swung open. Assorted clones sprinted out, firing at him. A hail of impacts of lasers and plasma bolts pounded into his ears as they burned the halls. Ronan swerved and sprinted, dropping grenades and sliding through the cleared door to the waiting room. Checking the locking mechanism as he hid around the side of the door's frame, he saw that the base of the door was burnt beyond any recognizable use, just a twisted metal base. Even if the electronic components worked, that wouldn't budge.

Flipping the switch on his plasma rifle, he sprayed plasma exhaust over the ceiling and the door to melt a barrier between himself and the clone army. The hallway became a small pneumatic tube filled with people, explosives, and one small window guarded by one angry space pirate. As molten metal flowed and dripped into a barricade, the numerous grenades in the hallway exploded. The ashes of his enemies exploded into Ronan's face.

After the dust settled, the saccharine muzak of the waiting room greeted Ronan. "I was hoping for smooth jazz," he lamented as he approached the front desk, took a knife off his bicep sheath, and shattered the glass. "Ready for this, you... fake human?" Ronan said to the mannequin, with a speaker in its chest, that sat in place of a receptionist. "Who runs this place?" he muttered. Then his calm snapped. "WHO THE HELL ARE YOU PEOPLE!?" he bellowed as ashes shook off his enraged face. "I've had it," he snarled. He kicked the door open and turned right down the hall to follow the path his friends walked the last time he saw them alive.

For a moment, the hallway remained silent. A door slid open and clones cautiously entered the hallway. "Change of tactics?" Ronan wondered, as he picked them off one by one.

The supersonic bolts of energy shrieked down the hall, burning each enemy beyond recognition. He advanced and then, suddenly, he felt horrible cramping, bringing him to one knee as he continued to cover himself behind a torrent of plasma.

He swung open the door to the restroom he'd visited a week ago, pulled a sidearm off his thigh to weld the doorframe shut, and reholstered it as he dragged himself into the stall. Sweat poured down his face and stung his eyes as venom and pain seeped through his digestive system. His head lolled and he could not move, hearing nothing but blood drip slowly into the water beneath him. Sticky with the sweat of illness, and powerless, he heard the pounding on the door progress from rhythmic drumming to a roar. The door clanged as the complex's numerous defenders battered their way in.

The misshapen horde of clones busted down the door and began firing at each closed stall. Fumbling with each of his holsters' straps and pulling up his pants, Ronan did not hesitate. He jumped through the stall and opened fire with both rifles, dropping six of the two dozen attackers. The rest crowded in on him, and he had no room to maneuver. He dropped the rifles, pulling his pistols. He twisted around the back of the closest assailant, firing at the two men in front of himself. A female clone leapt over their dead bodies. He swerved as she soared through the air to land on the clone he had previously juked. Without turning, he fired on them both.

Burning pieces of toilet paper floated through the air majestically as Ronan maneuvered around the room, alternately using clones as cover to block incoming laser shots and returning fire. He spun, his duster snapping through the air, before he slammed a boot into the face of an assailant, denting the marble along the wall with the clone's skull. As he opened fire at an assailant a foot in front of him, who collapsed in a heap, one of the nearly dead, scorched clones rose up and grabbed his gun arm, so Ronan dropped a knee into his throat and lifted the gun back up, the target now inches in front of him. The gun clicked empty. Dropping it, Ronan grabbed a supersonic knife and jumped into the attacker, driving the knife into his heart and shoving him through the doorway.

Having fought himself into position at another bottleneck, Ronan pulled two more of his pistols and fired up the light show. He did not stop until his weapons clicked empty. After a moment, only ashes floated in the air. He reloaded.

He punched the mirror with a gloved fist and used a shard to peek around the corner. All clear.

Ronan turned back to retrieve his rifles and reload his plentiful spare magazines into the emptied arsenal. Satisfied with his ammunition, he stormed out into the seemingly infinite hallway. As he sprinted forward and periodically stragglers would come out, but he put them down one after another.

He looked into one of the doors and saw cloning pods and

half-formed biological waste. He fought down bile in his throat and shot another clone in the face. He yelled, "KYLE! RICK! PETE!" and received no response. He scanned every doorway, seeing nothing but medical equipment, no storage of any dead bodies or restrained prisoners.

"Come on!" Ronan screamed. At this point he hadn't been assaulted for some time. His weapons glowed white hot. He opened another door only to find more medical equipment and a row of the sort of scooters he used to see the old and infirm riding in. "The hell?"

He slowed down to catch his breath and continued down the hallway.

A small doorway materialized. Slowing, he approached it.

He turned the bronze knob and swung it open, the other hand on his pistol. He saw row after row of test tubes, boiling liquids of various colors, and metal boxes laying on the floor like coffins, all in front of a tremendous central terminal with large screens and an array of buttons that lacked, to Ronan, any logical order. He walked over to the metal coffins, his breath catching in his throat. He pressed a red button on one of them, and the lid slid open. He stared down at an emaciated skeleton. Not one of his friends. "Abandoned victim," he feared.

He opened coffin after coffin, each one containing a corpse. He began to lose hope as he found only the dead. He activated every coffin on the left side of the room and moved to examine the right.

The third coffin squealed open. He found Kyle, who did not move. He lay flat on his back, his eyes closed. Numerous tubes stabbed into his body, half of them red with the blood they extracted. Ronan opened the other coffins in the same row and found his other two friends. Each of them lay still. Gingerly, he disengaged them from the tubes, applying pressure with bandages from his medikit to their multitudes of wounds. He worried more about whatever strange chemicals they might have absorbed than about the blood they'd lost.

He waited as they lay there. After a time, they stirred. They had not moved in a week, and muscle fatigue added to the weakness from the blood loss and the chemicals added to their bodies.

Rick could barely croak, "Water."

Pulling emergency rations from the medikit strapped to his thigh, Ronan gave each of them a small amount of water to wet their throats.

Slowly they each sat up. Pete looked down at himself. "Even alien kidnappers use these stupid hospital smocks?"

Rick eyed Ronan. "Where are we? What have they done to us?"

Ronan answered, "The Sperm Bank. Apparently it's a massive cloning operation. They weed people like me out with their little quality questionnaires and then they clone the best for some unknown purpose."

Rick began to chuckle before wincing. "Yeah, but you saved us."

They looked at their friend, Ronan, covered in soot and armed to the teeth. He said, "We shouldn't waste time. I have no idea how many more there are or what is even going on here. I have not seen a single alien, just an army of clones."

The captain asked, "Were any of them our clones?"

Ronan glanced at Rick, who was looking up under his thick eyebrows, steel in his gray eyes. "A lot of them."

Rick and the others did not want to hear more. "Before we go, I'd like to check the terminal," the captain said.

Ronan spun around, gasping, "What? We should get the hell out of here!"

Rick continued. "I want to know what they did to us. For all we know, they put bombs in us that'll explode when we get back to the ship."

Ronan replied, "I think we'll have to take that chance. We have no more time."

Rick held out a hand. "Just give me a quantum drive so we can download some info. I doubt five minutes will matter."

Ronan nodded and handed Rick the small universal hard drive. The captain approached the computer terminal under the massive wall-screen and pressed the drive to the computer, and nanobots streamed out to begin work. A shadowy face came into view onscreen. "You think your pitiful escape makes a difference?" it asked with a raspy voice, as if a scrap heap somehow managed to talk.

"What do you want?" Rick demanded.

"You will never know," it laughed.

Rick and the others stared at the screen. "I guess I don't really care. Anyway, I hope you're inside this station."

It scraped out another word. "Why?"

"I guess you'll never know." Rick grabbed the universal drive and gestured to Ronan, who shot the screen out in a blaze of plasma and glass shards. Rick smiled. "Got any portable nukes?"

Ronan laughed. "You're damn right I do." He pulled them out from his coat and placed them all over the lab.

Pete grabbed Ronan's arm, his grip noticeably enfeebled. "Wait, how do we get out in time?" he asked.

Ronan told him to hold on, and sprinted away from his confused friends. Wasting no time, he returned with his bounty. "I found these little old folks' scooters." He armed the nukes with a thirty-minute timer before they zoomed off like a geriatric biker gang.

Reaching the end of the hall, they were accosted by three clones: Kyle, Pete, and Rick. The Rick clone spoke. "How do you know your friends aren't clones? How do you know you saved anyone?"

Rick motioned to Ronan to hand him a pistol. The clones never flinched as they stared accusingly. Ronan looked from them to Rick, whose wan face showed no mercy. Ronan nodded to Rick and unholstered his piece. The Kyle clone said, "Come on, guys! Remember all my inappropriate comments?" Ronan flipped his pistol over to Rick's scooter. Still hunched over his handlebars, Rick caught it out of the air with one hand. The Rick clone asked again, shrillness creeping into his voice, "How will you ever know they're not the clones?" Plasma sizzled, and Rick shot all three dead.

They scootered past the smoldering corpses into the waiting room. Kyle noticed the charred remains of a mannequin. "That the receptionist?"

Ronan nodded.

"I wish we had the chance to kill her," Kyle lamented.

Ronan got off his scooter and handed them all weapons. "That's dark, man."

Pete scootered over to some magazines.

They all waited in front of the melted waste that blocked the hallway from the waiting room to the hangar. Flipping through a magazine, Pete asked disinterestedly, "Gonna blast us out?" He was answered by the blast of the plasma rifle.

Ronan, settling into his scooter, said, "Let's go."

Their scooters buzzed toward freedom, vibrating and shaking over the ruined hospital floor. "How much time do we have left?" Kyle asked Ronan.

"We have five minutes—let's go."

Near the end of the hall they had to get off the scooters because of all the corpses and debris littering the ground. They limped on, and Ronan scanned all open doorways for any more assailants. They left unimpeded.

Ronan began to worry. "Come on! We're running out of time!"

Rick yelled, "We're lucky we can even move. We'll make it!"

The entrance came into view and the *Morlaix* sat majestically before them, rusty patchwork hull and all.

Ronan helped them up the stairs into the airlock and ran toward the bridge. He disengaged the locking mechanism and began flying out, shooting lasers at the hangar bay doors to bust out. As they flew out of the hangar, his friends entered the bridge.

"No bare butts in the seats!" Rick coughed, grabbing the front of his hospital smock to remind everyone.

Standing at his post, Pete said, "Weapons charging."

Rick yelled, "View screen." They saw the many systems on the space station aiming towards them, and they could see batteries of weapons starting to glow with tremendous power.

Pete yelled, "They'll fire any second!" The weapons swerved and aimed. "THEY LOCKED ON!" Kyle screamed. "Brace for impact!"

The entire station exploded, its shock wave racing through the vacuum of space at them.

Kyle punched down on his terminal. "WARP US OUT OF HERE!"

Ronan fired up the engine, and they rattled as the shock from the numerous nuclear explosions reached them. Pieces of the station scraped their hull, but the engine engaged and they were traveling to safety far faster than any debris or shock wave.

They all took a breath. "We made it," Rick said, glancing up at his friend who'd saved them all. "How did you know they were clones anyway?"

Ronan laughed. "They didn't care about comfort, food, or our past." Rick raised an eyebrow as Ronan continued, "There was no passive-aggressive blame for our expulsion and eventual exile out into the deepest of space."

Rick responded, "Well, I don't think you have to worry about that anymore. How behind schedule are we on our latest delivery? We'll never get potatoes without it."

Ronan sat down heavily. "We're a week behind." He started unloading his arsenal. "But I think we'll make it."

Twentieth Century, Go to Sleep
by David Preyde

AT NOON I rolled out of bed in the clothes I'd worn for the last week, went downstairs, and checked e-mail. There was another message from my mother: *Jill, please call me. Or e-mail me. Or send me some indication that you're alive. I'm worried.*

Numb, I closed the laptop and went to the fridge to get breakfast. It was completely empty except for some leftover ice cream in the freezer from the night before. I stood in the kitchen, finished the ice cream, and then went back to bed for three hours.

I woke up with a splitting headache, which is what happens when you sleep for eighteen hours a day. Why couldn't I just sleep for the next fifty years?

But instead I drove to the grocery store. It was cold inside. Sterile. The lights overhead were too bright.

Pausing by the cucumbers, I noticed an elderly woman assessing me as if I was bruised produce. Was I imagining it?

That's what my therapist would say: It's all in your head.

Of course it's in my head, I wanted to say, That's why I need a therapist.

I felt my heart flutter and my gut stir. Warning signs. *I need to get out of here soon*, I thought.

But the only items in my cart were a cucumber, a stalk of celery, and French onion dip. I had to press on.

I went to the deli section, picked out chicken, steak and pork chops—no frozen dinners this week—glided through the chip and cookie aisle without pausing—God, I'm so good—and headed for the personal care aisle because I had run out of shampoo a month ago.

And there, not six feet ahead of me, was Henry, one of my students.

Well, former students.

Well, technically I might decide to go back to work at some point, let's not rule anything out.

He hadn't seen me yet.

I'd always liked Henry and had the sense that he liked me. He probably wasn't one of the kids responsible for spray painting *Miss Dempster is a fat whore* on the outside of the school gymnasium. But I'd gone on stress leave the next day and stopped answering calls and e-mails from the school, so I had no idea who was responsible, or if they'd even been caught.

"Miss Dempster, how are you?"

I spun around. It was Henry's mother.

"I'm fine," I said. "Just great."

"When are you planning to come back?" she asked.

Henry turned beet red. Embarrassed to be seen in public with his mother? Or embarrassed that his former teacher was a mess? It could be both.

Suddenly I was twelve-years-old again, on the playground during recess. I saw their leering, laughing faces. "Dumpster-Ass Dempster, Dumpster-Ass Dempster, Dumpster-Ass Dempster!"

I snapped back to the present. Henry's mom said, "Miss Dempster?"

"Yes, sorry, hopefully I can return to work soon."

I glanced at Henry, and he stared at the floor.

I abandoned my cart full of groceries and fled. I felt myself shaking and took stock. Anxiety: bad. Depression: off the charts. Feelings of guilt and shame: overwhelming. This would be a bad day.

It was twelve years ago that I graduated high school. Twelve years since my self-esteem was their property. But I kept remembering their faces, the things they called me.

That's the special gift of trauma; It turns you into a time traveler.

I HAD AN appointment with my therapist the next day. I was doing so badly that he probably felt like a failure. I wanted to make him feel better. So I showered and put on deodorant and my least dirty outfit.

The appointment did not go well.

"I'm worried that you're not engaging in the self-care practices we've talked about. I'm worried that you don't have a plan for your future."

Everyone's so goddamn worried about me, I thought. If they were really so worried, they'd help me achieve my dream of never getting out of bed again. They'd bring me a basket of groceries every week and periodically rotate me so I don't get a bedsore.

"I don't know what to say," I said. "Every time I go outside I have a panic attack. I just can't be around people."

The therapist sighed deeply and stared out the window.

"Take baby steps," he said. "If you don't like being around people, find something constructive to do outside the house that doesn't involve human contact."

"Like sacrificing a goat?"

He stared at me.

"I think we're done here," he said.

I DIDN'T DRIVE straight home. There was nothing there for me except Netflix, and it would wait like a loyal hound.

Maybe I should adopt an animal, I thought. But not a dog, they're too much work, and cats are mercenary psychopaths.

Maybe an iguana? Or a fish. I could buy an aquarium.

I drove past a billboard: *Self-storage facility for sale: 555-347-0078.*

Instead of going to the store and buying an aquarium and a bunch of useless fish, I pulled to the side of the road and took out my phone. It wasn't planned or anything. The idea occurred to me, so I just went for it.

A week later I was the proud owner of a slightly decrepit self-storage facility.

Located on the outskirts of town and consisting of two rows of prefabricated metal sheds and a shack by the gate, the facility had seen better days. There was a lot of rust and weeds.

But I figured it was easy money. People would pay me to keep their stuff safe, and since they paid through e-transfers I'd never even have to meet them.

I went to the hardware store and bought a ton of weed killer. I hired a contractor to repaint the sheds. I got my shack re-shingled and installed a space heater and a mini-fridge.

I still had to figure out how to get rid of all the raccoons that had moved into the vacant units. But, overall, I found myself in a state pretty close to happiness. I had a lot to think about and very few problems.

Weeks glided by like this, and I only had three panic attacks. I was even able to go to the grocery store and do some serious shopping.

One morning I got a call from a woman who told me her

dad was one of my tenants—is that the right word?—and he'd died. She wouldn't be paying for the unit going forward.

"What should I do with his stuff?" I asked.

"I don't even know what's in there," she said and hung up.

It didn't feel right to throw a stranger's possessions away. Who knew what priceless treasures I might find? Antique furniture. Beautiful crystalware.

The dead man's storage unit was at the end of the row: lucky number thirteen. I unlocked the door. Inside were two raccoons fucking. They hissed at me and ran away.

I was about to close the door again when I heard a rumbling sound from—no, that didn't make sense. The sound seemed to be coming from inside the far wall. It sounded like a train approaching. Part of me wanted to run, but instead I leaned forward, curious.

A flash of light erupted from the wall. I heard screams, and a young, gangly man lunged through the blast of hot brightness. He landed on his hands and knees and the light vanished, leaving behind no trace of anything unusual.

He panted heavily, head bowed, then staggered upward and dizzily grasped for a gun in his belt. He dropped it on the ground and vomited, then fell to his knees again.

"Are you okay?"

"Jesus," he said. "Jesus Christ." He took several deep breaths and stood up again. He made no move to grab the gun. "Wh-wh-where am I?"

"Hamilton."

He glanced at me, eyes full of fire. There was something else there, too. Fear.

"There's no Hamilton Street in Dallas," he said. "What're you talking about?"

"We're not in Dallas. Hamilton, Ontario."

He took a step forward and collapsed.

I knelt down and nudged him between his bony shoulders. He was pale and clammy. *Should I take him to the doctor's?*

As if he'd read my mind, he croaked, "No hospital. I won't be seen."

"Well…" I said. I had to do something.

I helped him stand and walked him back to my car.

"Where are we going?" he said, half-conscious.

"I'm taking you home."

"No," he said, "Please, I don't want to see Marina." I helped him into the back seat. "I can't see her, she'll kill me."

Then he fell asleep.

At home I was able to rouse the man from his stupor long enough to help him into the spare room and onto the sofa bed. I got him some Aspirin and a bottle of water, and, thinking about the gun, locked the door behind me.

What had that burst of light been? Some sort of portal? To where? The man thought he was in Dallas. Texas? I wasn't aware of any other Dallas.

But that was impossible. How would he have gotten from

Texas to Canada?

But here he was. *There must be some other explanation*, I thought. *This is ridiculous.*

I so badly wanted to call somebody and ask them for advice, or just tell them what had happened. But I'd lost touch with almost everyone in the last few years.

The last person to jump ship was Rachel. But I couldn't call her, not yet. Our breakup was still too fresh.

She'd know what to do. Or at least have some silly, smart-ass remark about the whole thing to make me feel better.

She'd always known how to keep me afloat, until it turned out that I'd been dragging her down. Those weren't her words, but that was the general idea.

I puttered around the house, cleaning, and it took most of the afternoon to make the place habitable. It had been a long time since I'd done housework. I didn't want to think about the stranger in the spare room or that peculiar burst of light.

After a few hours I heard the doorknob rattling.

"Hey," he said. "Hey! Let me out of here, goddammit!"

I rushed over and unlocked the door. He stumbled out.

"What the hell?" he said. "Where am I?"

"You're in my house in Hamilton, Ontario. And I locked the door because you have a gun."

He ran his hands through his greasy hair. "I'm not gonna shoot a woman," he said. "Christ, what do you think I am? Where's the latrine?"

I pointed him toward the bathroom and sat at the dining room table, waiting for him to emerge. When he finally did, he sat down at the other end.

"Thanks," he said. "For getting me away from the cops."

"You were being chased by the police?"

"Where you been? I killed Kennedy."

I laughed. I couldn't help it, it was so ridiculous. "Are you suggesting you're Lee Harvey Oswald?"

He shrugged, took out his wallet, and pushed it across the table. Inside was a driver's license with his face and name: Lee Harvey Oswald.

"There's a library card in there with my name on it too," he said.

I dropped the wallet.

"Okay lady, you gonna turn me in?" Lee stood. "Go ahead. I ain't gonna stop you. I don't want to turn you into an accessory or anything. You helped me out and I'm grateful. I'll tell the cops you didn't know who I was."

"It's not that," I said. "Well. Not *just* that. Do you know what date it is?"

"November 22nd."

"It's 2018."

He grinned, then stopped, arching an eyebrow, as though not understanding a punchline.

I grabbed the recycling bin full of old newspapers, snatched a few from the top, and dropped them in front of him.

Lee skimmed the front page, then another, and another, then looked up at me with that same quizzical expression.

"It's some kind of a gag," he said. "What do you want from me?"

I shrugged. "I don't know how this happened."

He stood, stomped to the bathroom, and slammed the door behind him, locking it.

Well, that's great, I thought. *What now?*

Lee stayed in the bathroom for hours. I knew he was in there, because it was windowless. And there weren't any sharp objects, so I knew he was safe. Unless he'd somehow been transported back to Dallas.

I went online and Googled "mysterious portal of light" and "time travel". Nothing helpful. I Googled "Lee Harvey Oswald".

I stopped, stunned.

According to Wikipedia, Lee Harvey Oswald had disappeared from the Texas Theater on November 22nd 1963 while being pursued by the police. The article claimed he'd never been apprehended.

What?

I kept Googling and found a galaxy of speculation and conspiracy theory about what had happened. There was even significant doubt as to whether he was the real killer.

I stared at the screen for a long time, trying to put it all together. Was I going crazy? Was this some 'roided out version of the Mandela Effect?

I Googled Jack Ruby. Nothing.

I picked up my phone and dialed Rachel. To hell with self-care and maintaining my distance and establishing healthy boundaries. If I was stranded in some alternate fucking universe, I had to hear the sound of her voice.

The phone rang and rang and went to voicemail.

I hung up and returned to the computer, trying to figure out what else had changed. I didn't notice any major differences, apart from the fact that an Oliver Stone directed biopic of Oswald had won a slew of Oscars in '91. I checked out Netflix to see if it was there—nope—and ended up watching several episodes of Buffy the Vampire Slayer. I couldn't think of a better response to the situation.

Lee unlocked the bathroom door and walked into the living room. "Do y'all still have cheeseburgers?" he said.

Fifteen minutes later I was driving through downtown with Lee Harvey Oswald in the passenger's seat. He was leaning his head out the window.

How do I even find myself in these situations? I thought. *Maybe this isn't even real, maybe I've finally cracked. I mean, I decided to let an honest-to-god assassin into my home, so I'm obviously not making the wisest choices. But am I floridly psychotic? How can you tell for sure?*

We stopped at a traffic light and Lee ducked his head back

into the car.

"This is unbelievable," he said. "The buildings are so weird."

You shot the President! I wanted to scream. How can you be so blasé about everything? The buildings are weird? How about the fact that you permanently altered the trajectory of American history?

Not to mention the trajectory of my personal history. Christ, have I committed a crime here? I'm harboring a fugitive.

I tried to imagine what would happen if I turned around and drove to the police station. What would they say? What would I say?

I kept driving. My head ached. I hadn't eaten all day, and a couple of cheeseburgers sounded like a good idea.

I pulled up in front of McDonald's. Inside, Lee stared at the menu, agog. "What's a 'McNugget'?" he said.

I glanced at him from the corner of my eye.

I'd been bullied from the time I was six-years-old. I knew how to read people, and I knew whether people were dangerous. I could always tell if someone were judging me, and whether they were going to express that judgement aloud or keep it to themselves.

And if they did say something I knew—just by looking at them—whether their motivation was to hurt me, or if they were genuinely ignorant.

When you're wounded that way, over and over, it can feel like life is whittling you down. But really, you're being carved into a blade.

"So how much am I allowed to get?" asked Lee. "Can I try out that McFlurry thing?"

I knew he wouldn't hurt me. That sounds crazy, but there was something about him I recognized. I couldn't quite put my finger on it. I'd seen that injured look in his eyes before, in the mirror.

In the end, Lee ordered two cheeseburgers with fries, ten McNuggets, an Oreo McFlurry, and a Coke. For the first time in a while, I was the one with less food on my plate.

We sat down, and Lee set into his meal like a ravenous dog.

"When was the last time you ate?" I asked.

He shrugged. "Yesterday, I think. Not sure."

He kept shoveling food into his mouth like he thought it might all disappear soon. Which made sense; he'd been ripped away from home and deposited in the future. What else was possible? I let him be and ate my own food.

Halfway through his nuggets, he smiled at me. "I don't even know your name."

"Jill Dempster."

"What do you do, Jill?"

"I'm a teacher. Was a teacher. I might still be, I'm not sure."

He grimaced. "I hated every teacher I ever had. What a waste of time." He ate a spoonful of McFlurry. "God, this is the best thing I've ever tasted."

After he finished his meal, we sat together in silence. Lee seemed fascinated by the people around us, craning his neck every which way, soaking up all the details.

"This is a weird place," he finally said, almost to himself, "seriously weird."

"I think we should talk," I said.

Lee's eyes locked onto me. "About?"

I hesitated.

"I know what you're going to say."

"I'm not turning you in," I said. "Because I don't know what would happen, and it kind of seems, well, pointless. But I don't know what the hell to do with you."

He relaxed, slouched back in his seat, and ran his hands through his hair. I caught an acrid pong of sweat.

"That makes two of us," said Lee. "Look, I'm not going to hurt you or anyone else. I don't want to cause any trouble. I did the hurt I meant to cause, and that's done."

"You can stay with me for a few days until we figure this out."

What the hell are you doing? I thought to myself. *You can't be friends with Lee Harvey Oswald.*

This isn't friendship, I argued. He needs help, and I can help him. How many times did *you* need help? How many

94

people have turned their backs on *you*?

You never committed murder, I replied.

If you don't think he deserves to be helped, then take him to the police right now.

Lee analyzed me, as if reading my thoughts.

"You're the nicest person I've met in a long time," he said. "Really."

Back home, I went online to see if anything else about the universe had changed. Try as I might, I couldn't find anything. For some reason that made me want to cry. Lee had disappeared from the face of the earth but nothing else had changed.

I also tried to phone Rachel several times but couldn't get through to her. She must be really pissed at me, I thought. I'd assumed we'd parted on good terms.

Lee spent a long time poring over my bookcases, taking books off shelves, flipping through them, and returning them to their original places. Finally he selected *Between the World and Me* by Ta-Nahesi Coates.

He flopped down on the couch and didn't move until he finished the book a few hours later. He disappeared into the spare room and turned off the light.

I tried phoning Rachel again. Nothing.

I'm going to have to figure this out myself, I thought. But I can't figure anything out right now. I went to bed.

Someone screamed—a wild, banshee cry—and I heard

glass smash on the floor.

I leapt out of bed, tore the door open, and stumbled into the living room. At the same time, Lee toppled out of the spare room, drenched in sweat.

"What's wrong?" I asked. His eyes skated across the room, taking everything in. "Lee."

"Had a nightmare. Woke up, wasn't sure where I was. I thought—But she would've died a long time ago."

He stared into space, then returned to his room.

The next morning, I slept in, woke at eleven, staggered through my morning routine, sat at the dining room table and poured myself some cereal.

At noon Lee emerged looking utterly wrecked, holding my copy of *Gone Girl*. He sat across from me, put the book down, and lay his head on the table.

"How'd you sleep?" I asked.

"I didn't," he croaked. "Around four, five a.m. I gave up and just decided to read."

"How'd you like the book?"

He looked up. "Oh it's good. I like these dime store novels. They take my mind off things." He noticed the cereal. "Where are your bowls?"

While Lee was fixing himself some cereal and toast, my cell phone buzzed.

It was the school. *Goddammit*, I thought. *What do they want?*

"Jill, hi. How- how are you?" It was Fred Coogan, the principal.

How was I? That was an excellent question. I hadn't experienced suicidal ideation for a few weeks, but Lee Harvey Oswald was eating Count Chocula at my breakfast table. All things considered, I'd say it was a wash.

"I'm doing fine. I think. What can I do for you?"

"Well, you can start by coming into work."

"Yeah," I said. "About that—"

"Look," said Fred, "I know you've been going through some things. And you've had challenges in the past, too. I know this. I'm not expecting you to just jump into your car and come to class today, but I'd like to have a conversation about this whole thing. If you can't do that, I'm afraid we'll have to involve the union."

My gut sank. I couldn't imagine going to that school. But I couldn't avoid it forever. Or could I? The self-storage facility was doing all right.

"Jill. Are you available in an hour?"

"Yeah. I can meet you then." I hung up.

"So that's what that thing is," said Lee. "A telephone."

What was I supposed to do with him? I didn't think he'd rob me or anything, but I felt a weird sense of responsibility for him.

"I have to go into work," I said. "Want to come with?"

"Don't you work in a school?"

"I swear it's not bad."

"If it's not that bad, why aren't you there right now? Isn't it a weekday?"

Fair point.

"You can wait outside, Lee. I mean, technically you're a fugitive, so you probably shouldn't be on school property anyway."

He smiled crookedly. "When we went to McDonalds, I kept waiting for people to recognize me," he said. "So far, nobody has."

"This really is the last place anyone is going to think of looking for you."

"All right, I'll come with. But can we go to a library after?"

A library? What for? I didn't want to ask, afraid there might be some sinister explanation. I offered him more Count Chocula.

My school was one of those buildings you wouldn't look twice at. Flat and beige, cradled on two sides by a parking lot.

I parked close to the playground and turned to Lee.

"Stay here, okay? I don't want anything weird happening."

"God forbid."

I took a deep breath, got out of the car, and walked slowly toward the front door, feeling like I was headed to my execution.

Fred Coogan's office was large, wood-panelled, and full of light. He sat behind an enormous desk, and stood when I entered.

"Jill," he grinned. "It is so good to see you. Please, have a seat."

I sat on the other side of the desk, and he sat too.

"Jill, this whole thing…" He trailed off. "I want to apologize on behalf of the school. I also have a letter of apology written by the students responsible. They were suspended for two weeks. We took this situation very seriously."

I bowed my head, not sure what to say.

"I know you've had difficulties in the past," said Fred. "That kind of stuff, you know, it's hard to deal with. I know as well as anyone. I've had setbacks. Everyone has setbacks. But it isn't about how many times you get knocked down. It's how many times you get back up."

He smiled, so pleased with the person he believed himself to be.

"You gotta get back up, Jill. That's all there is to it. And I know if you have the right attitude, you can beat this thing. Jill, I know you."

"That's it, huh?" I said.

"That's it."

Did Fred really think he could solve my mental illness just by talking at me? Of course he did. He was the guy who got things done.

I felt my face grow hot. I didn't want anyone to know me, to really see me.

"You're funny. You throw up these walls to keep people out. You don't have to do that. You don't have to pretend."

My breathing grew shallow: a warning sign.

"We're here for you. All of us here at the school, we're a family. We'll support you until you find that light at the end of the tunnel. Just talk to us, any time." He drummed his fingers on the desk. "But no more hiding."

I nodded and bit my lip.

Don't cry, I thought, *not here.*

"So we'll see you on Monday," said Fred, as if that was decided. "It'll be a fresh start."

I got up and drifted back to the car. Lee sat in the front seat, watching a couple of kids playing in the schoolyard. He glanced at me when I sat behind the wheel.

"I can't hear what they're saying," he said. "But I know exactly what's being said. I remember it all so clearly. What it was like to be a kid. Sometimes I still feel like I'm back there."

He glanced at me again, and must've seen that my eyes were red. His expression changed. "Jill, you okay?"

"Oh, I'm doing great," I said. "Top of the world."

"You want me to burn this place down?"

I laughed, then realized he wasn't joking. "That'd probably be an overreaction, Lee." I wiped my eyes. "It's just—God, things are a mess."

Lee continued watching the kids in the yard, and I did too. A bigger kid pushed a smaller one into the sandbox and pulled a toy truck out of his hands.

"I went to a lot of different schools as a kid," said Lee. "I wanted to burn every one of them down. But I couldn't figure out how to do it. That's what I used to think about when the teachers put a switch on me."

"Did that happen a lot?" I asked.

"All the time. It didn't work for me though. I just laughed. It didn't hurt at all compared to what some of my mom's boyfriends did to me." Lee looked over at me and shrugged. "What about you? Did you get the switch in school?"

"They don't do corporal punishment any more, Lee. It's against the rules."

"Shit," he said, "I knew I was born ahead of my time."

"I did all right in school. With the teachers at least. Not so much with the other kids. They used to make fun of me. I didn't want to tell anyone—the teachers or my parents—because I didn't think they'd be able to stop it. They didn't even know it was happening, and it was happening at least—God, at least thirty times a day. If the adults were that oblivious, how could they have possibly helped?"

The school bell rang, piercing and metallic.

"It's funny, isn't it," said Lee. "You think you've grown up and moved on. And for a while you do okay, but then something happens and all the old feelings return. And you're back where you started. I can't figure out how to live with that." Lee continued staring out the windshield at the schoolyard, now empty.

I drove out onto the road and Lee said softly, "The past is a light sleeper."

We pulled up in the parking lot of the library.

"I've just got to ask before we go in. Why are we here?"

Lee frowned and cocked his head. "Jill, you're telling me that if you traveled more than fifty years into the future you wouldn't want to see a library?"

Okay, fair enough.

We walked through the front doors together and stood in a glass atrium that stretched four stories above our heads.

"Where's the card catalog?"

It took me a second. "Oh. We don't have those anymore. Come here, I'll show you."

Lee obediently followed me into a large chamber filled with rows of computers. We found an empty seat near the back.

"Sit here," I said. "I don't know how well I can explain this to you. But this is a computer."

He brushed the keyboard with his fingers.

"Like a typewriter?"

"It's a typewriter that's hooked up to a card catalog. You type in the book or author you're looking for right here, you see? And then you hit enter, and the screen will show you where in the library you can find what you're looking for."

"Crazy," said Lee. "Can this computer do anything else?"

I hesitated. How much should I tell him?

"It hooks up to the Internet. That's like—well, it has pretty much all the information you could want. About anything."

Lee stared at me. "You're joking."

I realized what I had just told him, and how extraordinary it must seem.

"You have to show me how it works."

I wasn't sure where to start, so I pulled up Google.

"This is—I don't know, I guess you could call it an oracle. Ask it anything you want."

"Anything?"

"Anything. I'm going to, uh, I'm going to check out some books, okay?"

And then I left Lee with access to all the world's information. It occurred to me that this might not be the best idea. I mean, I was majorly fucking with history, right? But Lee was trapped in the twenty-first century. He might as well have as much information as possible about it.

Still, I was nervous. After browsing through the shelf of newly acquired books, I went back to check on him. He sat staring at the computer screen, hands folded in his lap.

"Lee?" I said. I looked over his shoulder.

He had found a news article. At the top of the page was a black and white photograph of a beautiful young woman with a pensive face. The headline: *Whatever happened to Marina Oswald?*

"Is that—"

"My wife."

"I didn't know you were married."

"With two kids." His eyes shone with tears. "Jill, I don't know how to get home. You've gotta help me."

We drove through residential streets, heading back to the storage facility. I had no idea whether the portal could still be accessed. Somehow I doubted it.

Lee stared out the window.

"What did the article say, Lee? Is your family okay?"

"They're fine," he said, his voice deliberately light. "Marina got married again. My girls didn't even know I was their dad until they were grown."

"I'm sorry."

"No. That's me, that's always been me. Looking for a way to set the school on fire."

We passed a field of transmission towers and a shabby strip mall.

"She told the reporter she wasn't sure if I'd, uh, if I'd ever loved her. That, if I really loved her and the girls, I wouldn't have killed Jack."

I stole a glance at him, afraid to ask the question.

"Lee… why did you do it?"

"I don't know," he said. "It wasn't, like, planned out or anything. I don't do plans, really. Ideas occur to me and I just go for it. I proposed to my wife the second time we met. I didn't even love her yet, that came later. I just wanted to see what she'd say." He smiled, and then it faded. He bit his bottom lip. "I heard Jack was coming to town, and something went off inside me. I never had a problem with his politics. Hell, I even voted for him. But the kind of man he was is the opposite of me. I can't properly explain it."

I parked outside locker number thirteen. I wasn't sure how much to tell Lee about what waited for him in 1963.

"If you go back you'll get arrested. You might not see your family again."

"I was hiding from the cops in a theatre when I ended up here. If I can run from them just a little longer, I can get home and apologize to Marina. The girls are at school, but maybe I'll have time to write them a note."

I knew that wouldn't happen. Lee would be cornered in the theatre and arrested. Two days later, he'd meet Jack Ruby.

Strange, I thought, looking at Lee. He was so healthy and so alive. But he had only two days to live.

"I'll come with," I said.

"What are you talking about?"

"I'll talk to the police. Provide you with an alibi. Maybe it'll work, maybe it won't, but I can at least delay things a bit. Give you a chance to talk with your family."

Lee looked at me, puzzled. "You'd go to 1963 for me."

"What else have I got going on? I can spend a few days in the past. I've lived most of my life there anyway. It's not like

I'm ever going back to work."

Lee shrugged. "I'm not in the habit of telling people what to do with their lives. You can come if you want."

"That's a great way to thank me for trying to save your neck."

He locked eyes with me, took my hand, and squeezed it.

"Thank you, Jill. I mean it."

I unlocked the door. No raccoons this time. The back wall was quiet and still. Lee and I stood next to it for a while, waiting.

"What do we do?" said Lee.

"I don't know. I was just standing here and I heard a sound and then you came through."

"Maybe it only goes in one direction," said Lee, "We should—"

A noise, different from the last time. It sounded like rushing, cascading water. Then I was sucked forward through the wall, and felt a blast of icy cold.

My head pounded. I lay on concrete dusted with snow. Lee was next to me, on his hands and knees, dazed.

My head quickly cleared and I managed to stand. Lee too.

"It's not as bad this time," he said. "Maybe going backward is easier than going forward."

"I'll mention that to my therapist." I glanced around. "Where are we?"

We were in a park, surrounded by bare trees and dead

grass. Snow swirled lightly in the frozen night air. About a block away I spotted a towering grey building.

"This isn't Dallas," said Lee. "I think it's New York." He stepped forward and looked around. "This is Central Park. I was here a few years ago."

"How the fuck did we end up in New York?" I said. "And *when* are we? It feels like the middle of winter."

We walked toward the street and, passing a newsstand on the corner, I peered at the date of The New York Times: December 8th 1980. Then I looked up and realized we were standing across the street from the Dakota.

Oh, shit.

"What's wrong?" said Lee. "It looks like you've seen—"

"John Lennon's about to be murdered," I said.

I pulled him by the arm into a bus shelter, not wanting to be overheard by the people passing us on the sidewalk. Even in New York, this was not a normal conversation.

"John Lennon—like, from The Beatles?" said Lee. "The band that did *Love Me Do*? Why would anyone murder him?"

"They end up being kind of a big deal. They're like—the Shakespeares of rock 'n roll, okay? And John Lennon wasn't just a musician. He was an activist. Really politically in-volved—"

That got Lee's attention. "What did he believe in?"

"No war, no poverty, no prejudice, no religion. He claimed not to want material goods either, but Christ, look at where he's living. On December 8, 1980, he was gunned down outside of his house—that apartment building right there."

Lee stared at the Dakota, assessing it, digesting what I'd told him. "Does he have a family?"

"Yeah, he has a wife. She's an activist, too. And a son. He's five-years-old."

He turned and walked toward the Dakota. I followed. "Lee, what are you doing?"

He spun around to face me, walking backwards.

"I'm going to save him, Jill. Don't talk me out of it. Don't give me a chance to think. I've got to do this. What else could I do?"

There was some truth to that. If he went back to 1963, he would die. If he went to 2017, how could he possibly build a life for himself? Trying to disarm John Lennon's assassin was risky, but maybe it could work.

"I'm not in the habit of telling people what to do with their lives," I said. "You can go if you want."

He let loose a wild, dangerous grin. Still walking backwards, he spread his arms out. "What'll they think of me now?" he cried.

He turned and ran across the street, around the corner of the Dakota.

Who is 'they'? I thought.

The light changed, and I was forced to wait as cars rushed past. The wind blew through me. As soon as I could, I ran across the street. I approached the corner of the building and heard a gunshot.

I turned the corner. Lee lay on the pavement. Dead. John Lennon and Yoko Ono crouched next to him.

And standing between them and me was Mark David Chapman, gun in hand. He dropped the gun and ran.

A thought occurred to me, and I pursued him.

Mark ran through traffic. Cars squealed to a stop. I still followed. He ran into the park. I couldn't let him go. A painful stitch coursed up my side. I couldn't run much longer.

"Mark!" I called.

He stopped and turned, tilted his head, puzzled. I could see the questions in his eyes: how did I know his name? Who was I?

I extended my hand. "Come with me. I know a way out."

Leavings of the Smooth World

by Leonie Skye

THIS BODY SITS down in a corner and freezes, stiff black sleeves glued to red velvet chair arms.

Cradle AI must be powering down unnecessary mobility in light of the new energy savings rules.

Within these now-static eye sockets I make fine adjustments to the ciliary muscles and regard the sandwich sitting on a chunky antique table off to the side. Ham and Swiss, I believe. Smell is still on, so the aroma creeps enticingly into these nostrils. But I can't lift an arm to get it.

Peripheral vision shows a fire-lit, extravagantly draped, and heavy wood interior, and the lap of this body, clothed in a maid's uniform. The back is erect, and I know I left the facial expression loyal and attentive.

I assess. Mobility is unlikely to return in the last eight minutes of my shift because the Master Body—now erotically engaged with two rainbow-colored Lithe Things—won't need me for a while.

The Union won us the right to remain in the Smooth

World with Sight, Smell, and Hearing switched on during downtime. So I could just wait until the end of my shift. It's considered a privilege to watch the Master Bodies do... whatever they might be doing.

But once I was prevented from shutting the eyes as my Master Body ate one of the rainbow-colored Lithe Things like a chocolate bar, peeling and crumpling the colorful skin, biting into the chalky smoothness, and releasing a gush of dark red sludge, perhaps raspberry flavored.

Right. Time to latch out while I still can. If it needs anything, it can call me back.

I close the eyes. With an old-fashioned clink and whoosh, the room, with its writhing bodies, squeezes down to a gray dot. As the two-way electrical stream slows to a trickle, and my actual body and the Smooth World pull out of each other, my pod's six gray padded walls materialize. I unlatch from all the wall drives, pulling gently so the hair-thin cords glide back under my skin.

Smell and Taste are sort of a liability. Originally, attendants had been permitted only Sight, Hearing, and Touch, just enough for the work really. But when I started, the Union had just won Taste and Smell.

I run four capabilities in the Smooth World—Mobility and Muscle Endurance (I can stay upright for days), Feelings (circumscribed to shame and loyalty), Problem-Solving (in case something goes awry in a way not purchased by the

Master Body), and Senses (Sight. Hearing. Taste. Smell. Limited touch. In other words, I would have been able to savor that sandwich).

The problems of perfect attentional intersubjectivity and the biocompatibility of electrode housing were solved decades before I was conceived. So going on shift is less like walking through a door and more like allowing the Master Body's particular Smooth World to penetrate me and rush into areas of my brain and extended nervous system through embedded neural prostheses.

When I synch up, I understand the world just exactly as the Master Body does. Its desires, its politics even. I can see and feel the world it's built for itself out of staggeringly expensive experiential packages, recent add-ons, and its own copyrighted sensations. I can manipulate this middle-aged female attendant body as an adjunct to that world, vocalizing, feeling, and thinking within constraints.

Consequently, there are always a few moments of an ashamed hunger that lingers after I unlatch, a self entirely bent toward the Master Body, waiting to serve it but also wanting what it has and waiting to snatch up what it might leave behind. Yet still feeling loyalty and craving approval.

These tendencies gradually dissolve as I lie there and the full, sparse reality of my own life rushes back into where the neural hook-ups prevented it from nesting. The sandwich becomes an abstract idea.

I stretch my fingers apart and call up my schedule. Good. Unless the Master Body calls me back into service in the next seven minutes, I'm on break. Knowing what I do of its predilections, I figure I'm free for the next twenty-four hours and seven minutes.

I turn my hands down and rest my palms on the rough cotton sheets of my pod bed. I lift a leg and run my toes down the padding and extruded plastic of the walls.

I put my hand down my thin cotton pants, and my clitoris blooms. My brain stumbles around searching for images, either in the Smooth World or the Cradle. Honestly, the Lithe Things do nothing for me. Instead, I think about Alex, from the canteen. There's something about her grin and the wrinkles at the corners of her light brown eyes.

I also think of wet, green grass, and what I can recall of a type of white, sweet flower I smelled once, long ago. I come quickly, bracing against the close walls, trying not to knock too hard or vocalize too much.

Then I sit up, fan my face, and slip on shoes. I key the door aside and step out into the putty-colored corridor.

"SHE DIDN'T GET it." Annie gestures at the unchanged code. "Look."

"Cradle AI powered down mobility…" Denny reads back through the code. "Seven minutes before the end of her shift.

Why?"

The hum of the servers washes in. Annie puts her latte down and leans over Denny's shoulder. "Does it... know?"

Denny presses his eyes with the heels of his hands and says, "Whether it knows or not, Annie, we don't have much time. That's for darn tootin'."

I CAN NEVER resist, even though this little-used outer corridor is hotter than hell. I stop at the large, gray, rectangular screen and press my fingers to it. Aroused, it bleeds a picture onto its surface. Not just a picture. The actual outside world. When on break, I can stare at it for hours of my precious time.

A deep, dark blue, what they call—what is *actually*—sky blue. Under it sits a mountain, faceted, diversely textured, a myriad browns, some you might even allow as red, some you'd call gray, and everything in between.

It's a wildness of color that exists inside the Cradle only on skin or in eyes. I wonder what's still alive up there, burrowed into the hard soil, coolish under rocks, or thriving at the heart of thick, tough agaves, and waiting until the nighttime temperature becomes a livable 115° or so.

It's also a familial thing, this view. It's approximately the same as that from my great-grandparents' back window. It's the backdrop to their kidney-shaped pool and terra-cotta potted flowers, the round black barbecue, all gone now. But I saw these things once in real life, when I was very little.

Now it's just part of my fund of experiences, bequeathed to me, protected by property law. That precise experiential package, that collection of memories, my family's sensorial footprint, so to speak, can be changed to code, and I'll synch up to it as a full agent with all rights. Some day.

My relationship with Alex has gotten only so far as sharing some of our funds. Alex lets me see pictures of an old family dog her grandmother once had. Viewing it, a living creature was somehow conjured, warm, wiggling, and soft, though I'd never held a dog myself. Alex said this dog would definitely be in her Smooth World.

I showed her a photograph of the view out the back window onto the potted flowers, my great grandfather floating in the pool, sun blinking off his sunglasses, that mountain in the background. Together, we'd puzzled through the richness of these things, imagining. Afterward, she'd brushed my hand with her fingertips.

Under the mountain, as far as the lens can see, are the begging palms of the solar panels that power the Cradle as well as Desert Sunset. Plunked halfway up the foothills, Desert Sunset is a series of linked, partially-submerged white boxes where the Smooth World was built and where the engineers live.

Cradle AI is just now turning the palms to catch the sun's last angle before it dips behind the mountain. Their shadows are a poor substitute for those of a flock of birds.

I hear the chants of the Etherists' concluding prayer humming through the walls: "We await the loving arms of the almighty Smooth World, and pray for acceptance into its sensorial paradise for as long as we are worthy."

We have two religions in the Cradle. Etherist and Dimensionalist.

As I understand it, the Etherists believe the original marketing from TV. The ads said that when the cradle falls, as people like to joke, we will all climb into our pods, latch in, and live in the Smooth World, "experiencing" whatever it is we have been able to afford, until our actual bodies give way and disintegrate into our sealed-up pods. But we won't notice. We will simply blink out and go gently, even happily.

However, some of the crazier Etherists seem to believe the sensorial sophistication we've achieved through SenseXML—which drives our Smooth World integration—can make us live well past when we should, by tricking our senses and the biological processes they trigger, into thinking us fed and nurtured, perhaps forever.

Personally, I think those folks have a poor grasp of science. When we're all latched in, no one's going to be filling feeding tubes or hydration lines like some of us workers do for the Master Bodies. Though the Master Bodies weren't rich enough for the floating nation-state, or "barge" as some call it, they *could* afford permanence in the Smooth World, lots of space on the server, and a team of attendants to maintain their bodies.

But lots of people don't have the funds yet to carve even a paltry spot in the Smooth World. Me, for example. I have a rich fund of experiences, for sure, but I own no server real estate. It will take me, oh, perhaps ten more years at the least, to purchase the space and the code to make that view of the flowers, the pool, my great-grandfather, and the mountain an experience I can actually realize as *mine*.

Now the Dimensionalists' take on everything is far weirder. They believe fervently that the Smooth World—that immense, twisting, branching forest of code—has essentially gone rogue. In the beginning it was just a complex set of commands to help rich people wrap themselves in pleasantly ordinary earthly experiences as the real world heated up and went underwater.

But now, they believe, the Smooth World has taken itself over, become intelligent, and hatched another dimension beyond itself. Something real. And it is there that we will all go.

How, though? The Dimensionalists believe there are holes, pathways, blown open by experiences so sharp and sensorially ecstatic that they can propel one into that world beyond the Smooth World but *of* the Smooth World. Something new made from the pieces of the world we all craved as this one was dying, and even sprouting new, heretofore unseen, unfelt things up out of its figurative soil, of its own design. Things of which no one has ever even heard.

Whew! I don't know, honestly. I can't quite disentangle what any of this means for me. In a way I'm with the Atheists and Unionists. Just let us all have equal access to roam in the Smooth World, and we can all see what happens. Heaven knows I'd love it if I could just punch through my Master Body's stupid, gothic bedroom somehow or just walk out a door. Seriously, it never does anything but skulk around that dark room, ordering me around. The place smells from all its exertion. I really pulled a short straw. I've been trying for about the last three years to get shifted to a new Master Body.

But at the moment, my only true religion is Alex.

Reminded of her, I pull my fingers off the screen and take a sharp right down another putty-colored corridor. On her downtime she likes to hang in the canteen and play chess. When I find her there, sitting with a small crowd of other players, I feel lucky.

She sees me and waves.

I hang out at the edge of her circle, with a variety of Cradle folks who watch the game, drink tequila, pop protein pills, and, of course, touch each other. Arms drape across shoulders, hands are held, hair is gently brushed from cheeks or foreheads.

These arms, these fingers, these cheeks are a variety of hues, from a deep dark brown that I think was once called black, the color of the mountain just after sunset, to something I think was once called white, the color of the walls of the Cradle corridors, or the sun-blasted ground under the solar panels.

Headquarters has encouraged us to call ourselves only Cradle Dwellers, though. It says we should be "post-hue." We are all one, says official doctrine. We are all patriotic servants of the United States of America, what's left of it.

"Fuck that shit," Alex likes to say. "I'm brown Chicanx. Fuckers can't take that away."

I'm thinking about pushing through the crowd and being so bold as to sit next to her, when the Headquarters screen blinks on. It takes up an entire wall of the cavernous old warehouse that houses the canteen and other common spaces. As it lights our faces with its projection of real colors and forms, it catches the edge of the sign of what this place used to be, before it was stitched together with all the other warehouses of the quadrant and repurposed as the Cradle. The mysterious, ancient word "Costco" is bathed in light, and I'd rather just stare at that than at what's on the screen.

"THEY'RE HERE, ANNIE," says Denny. "Do you want to do this here? Or..."

"Here's fine," Annie says, sitting up straight and gesturing toward the empty seats.

The Archivists pull them up to Annie's couch. The seats are low-slung, blond wood. The couch is a tasteful charcoal gray, something old from the last modernist resurrection, but comfortable. The sun is setting, so Denny pulls the double shade back, exposing the triple-paned glass. The Archivists, Annie, and Denny take a moment to look out past the shadows of the long eaves.

Still beautiful, Annie thinks. This burning place, Quadrant 89, which was once, many years ago, called Tucson, Arizona. But what was once a city is just a sprawling pile of barely recognizable building rubble now, bones bleached, softer tissue gone to dust.

One of the Archivists clears his throat.

"Yes," Annie says. "You may begin if you like."

"Thank you. We appreciate your cooperation."

She nods, and there's a long, preambling silence.

"You're a legend," says the other Archivist finally. "An artist."

Annie laughs. "Is that so?"

"You practically built the Smooth World."

"Rubbish," she says. "The coders did."

One of the Archivists begins writing.

Annie wrinkles her brow. "Where will these scribblings be placed?"

"They'll be sealed up in the Cradle. Tonight. For any future civilizations or visitors. Yours is the last interview, and there's a rover ready to transport all the hard documents after we're done. Exciting."

Annie stares at the man, and he clears his throat and looks down at a pad of paper.

"Let's start at the beginning. You were hired part-time to—"

"Hunt for funny pixels, for crude steganography," she says. "Back then, we still had an open internet, and the Rough World was sending coded messages in images and video. I was hired to search for odd configurations of pixels, things that didn't make sense. I'd take a suspicious swatch and send it on over to Analysis. They'd hit it with their statistical methods and go fishing, see if they could pull a ghost image or message out of the pixel ocean. We crushed their communications. We crushed the resistance."

Denny chimes in. "Annie has an extraordinary ability to go low, as they say. Possibly the keenest ever recorded. Sees the parts of things and is able to ignore the big picture."

"I have weak central coherence," she adds.

"Though we like to say she has *strong* attention to fine detail." Denny reaches over and squeezes her shoulder, which she lifts affectionately in response.

"I don't get distracted by laws of global precedence, gestalt laws, like neurotypicals do. I can—*could* see where the pixels didn't make sense. Where things might be hiding. But that was long ago."

Both Archivists are scribbling away. One asks, "And is that

what led to your development of the Smooth World? That… attention to detail? Is that how you got hired as a creative?"

"Hah! I told you. Denny here… and the others, they did the work. They put it all into code. It was already mostly built when I came to work here. I just needed a part-time gig to put food on the table."

"But you're the one who really made it what it *is*. Without you, it never would have been so detailed. So sensuous. So real. It was after you started introducing things like… the texture of coffee grounds on the tongue, the pressurized feel of being underwater, the sensation of a purring cat on a lap, or the way a setting sun catches leaves or—just things no one had thought to remember."

"Yes, well, we have my sister Sarah to thank for that."

The heads of the Archivists snap up. "The terrorist?"

She ignores the question. "She was a philosopher, highly educated. Rather useless in that era, true. But she told me life is just a collection of culturally-organized sensuous moments, some pleasant, some painful. I said, Well then, the Smooth World needs to be just that, sensuously detailed. My family had a lot to work with, so I mined that first. I mined *our lives*."

Annie gets lost remembering how they'd all sit out back of the house by the pool as the sun was setting. Then late into the evening, catching the last of the cool evening breezes, they'd all talk about their favorite experiences and what they wanted to see replicated in the Smooth World.

Her mother had wanted the icy springtime creeks of Wyoming, warm sunlight glancing off and drying her wet arms. Horses that feel strong and warm between legs. The Left Bank of Paris with its smelly cobblestone alleys, wine bars, and harsh cigarette smoke. The Dutch masters of the Louvre perfectly lit, the air swimming with dust motes, and the Sorbonne exact down to the last poorly-erased chalkboard. The Coup de Choux all dark, candle-lit, smelling of coq au vin. Paperwhites, the cool of a pressed tablecloth under your palms in a quiet restaurant, the way red wine catches light as you pour it, the way strong coffee pries open your brain, warm terra cotta, the Alhambra.

Her dad had desired the smells of engine grease, printer ink, and hot paving materials. The clean, cool press of a good steel pen in the hand, the crack of a hank of paper slapped down on a wood table, the black, shiny curl of lead from the edge of a palm to the side of a pinky.

Before disappearing, Sarah had grudgingly come up with some funny ones. That feeling of blowing one's nose satisfactorily. The muted rattle of subway cars in an underground movie theater. The feeling of humming calm that spreads through your legs after a run. The vibrating warmth of a tiny newborn.

For her part, Annie had been lucky. She'd seen Tokyo, Addis Ababa, Paris, Istanbul, Vienna, Berlin, Beijing, Reykjavík, Lima, Mexico City, Dakar, Johannesburg, and more.

She'd swum in oceans, hiked mountains, flown in aircraft, before such things went away. She'd sat in sweltering plazas drinking ice-cold beer, choked on the charred-meat smoke of covered markets, ice-skated on frozen rivers, bit into overripe tropical fruits, juice running between fingers.

All of these experiences now resided in delicate, fine code. Simulacra of a billion worlds spun up and gathered by a billion different perspectives. The Smooth World.

Annie looks over her shoulder and realizes that the stars have come out and there's only a fine orange glow at the rim of the Santa Catalinas. It has the look of coolness even if it isn't cool. *We had so much*, she thinks.

She doesn't tell the Archivists about how she has carefully set aside many of these sensorial swatches for her grand-niece, complete with photographs, recordings, and faithful poetic descriptions, though she knows the girl can't read. Surely someone will read them to her? Annie had had them copyrighted, back when experiences were becoming privatized, monetized.

All for naught, she thinks now. The kid has nothing, no money for server space and code. Hardly anyone has enough money to afford these increasingly scarce resources because there's no more space for data centers, no more materials to make the chips and boards and casings, and the maintenance and governance of data is impossible in a world where most people who can afford it have checked themselves into the

Smooth World anyway.

Leia has a rich fund of material, sure, but no way to translate it into experience. She's just an attendant, and Annie knows, from watching the code, that hers is a shitty Master Body, cruel and boring.

It's time to bring her through if we can, she thinks. *Last chance.*

"Excuse me, gentlemen. I'm afraid I'm weary. Past my bedtime." She stands and supports herself on Denny's wheelchair as they clasp hands and head for the door.

"GOOD EVENING, CRADLE Dwellers," says the Supreme Leader.

My eyes are screwed tight to the mysterious word, Costco. Ever since Alex taught me how to read it, I've been trying to figure out how letters work. I'm sorry to say that they still mostly elude me, though the word "Alex" makes sense—*al ex*, simple. But I can make out a large, orangeish blob of an individual, some light hair blowing in a breeze. He's outside. *Outside.* Imagine that. Surrounded by a blue, shifting expanse. Ocean water. It looks cool there, wherever it is.

"I'm going to be straight with you," the figure says.

I feel someone take my hand. It's Alex. My chest goes all fluttery. So I stare at her or at my feet for the rest of it.

"We're going to be making some changes."

You can feel a tightening all around, everyone clenching

their stomachs and jaws at once. "Oh yeah, *pendejo*?" whispers Alex beside me. I squeeze her hand.

"I have determined that we spend too much—*far* too much on some of our Cradles. And as you know, we are facing possibly the greatest threat we've ever known in the form of ocean-going terrorism. These are horrible people who have nothing but contempt for our way of life and must be destroyed at all costs. As all available resources must be turned to this effort, we can no longer afford the very very wasteful expenditure of paying *live* attendants for the Master Bodies or provisioning unproductive Cradles with food and medicine. Local sustainability has always been the goal of my administration, and we are about to get very serious about it. There will no longer be costly subsidies paid for by our tax dollars. Smooth World attendance will be transitioned over to AI, and I have even directed my Commander of Land Quadrant Operations to select five of the Cradles to be mothballed at…" There's a collective gasp. "Midnight, Desert Sunset time."

Alex looks in my eyes.

"Tonight?" someone shouts. Panicked murmuring rises from the crowd.

"Which ones?" someone else calls.

"You may now be wondering which Cradles have been selected," the voice drones. "To be as humane as possible, I have directed my commander not to release this information before the changes have been made. Therefore—*therefore*…"

We stand in stunned silence. The Supreme Leader is all alone, I can see now that I force myself to look at him. He's standing on the deck of the barge he has been living on since the capital went under water. He lives there with the handful of people who could afford to buy physical space on the floating nation-state in addition to access to the Smooth World. He's wearing a comfortable-looking pair of beige pants and a bright blue short-sleeved shirt.

"*All* Cradle Dwellers must either go into the Smooth Worlds they have purchased or report for duty with their Master Bodies by twenty-three hundred hours Desert Sunset time. If your Cradle has not been selected, you will be able to latch back out again at twenty-four hundred hours. If not..." He pauses here and grins, lifts his chin. "Look, my fellow Americans. This is the moment we've been preparing for. We have the greatest Smooth World in the world. We have the most fabulous, the best coders in the world. Simply put, we have the best *new* reality. Latch in and live the dream. Latch in and *serve* the dream one last time. We're relying on your patriotism."

The image fizzes out.

"What the fuck?" someone whispers right next to me. It's not Alex. It's a young man clutching a bunch of protein pills in both fists and wetting himself.

Alex pulls me to her. "Come on," she says.

"Look at it, Den," Annie whispers. "It's sort of beautiful. Sort of scary."

"Hmm, I suppose."

Annie watches lines of code pouring down a screen, cascading, intertwining across the three-dimensional visual depth of the monitor. She knows they're only looking at the tip—the "tit", as Denny likes to say—of the iceberg. It roils around, chasing its own tails, swallowing itself, regurgitating, recycling. It's knitting, crocheting. It's braiding and looping, cross-stitching, purling, and cat-cradling. It's taking the strands and kneading them, punching them, stretching them, winding them around themselves, then tossing it all in the air.

"But can it save us? Can it save *her*?"

"Well, fuck me if I'm gonna have a philosophical conversation right now, love, but... I'm not sure it'll be *us*, or *her* necessarily."

"But it'll be something... a life of sorts."

"It'll be something, that's for sure."

Union people are spreading through the crowd. Everyone wants to know what happens to those of us without server space, of course.

"It's time," the union people respond, with a bewildered

tone. "Time to grab what you can, what belongs to the people."

This muted revolutionary command merges somehow with a Dimensionalist message going around, that partaking of some sensorial experience during your next shift—even if you have to steal it—will launch you into the world beyond the Smooth World, that unknown promised land. So use your neural prostheses! Take a sip of something strong, burn your attendant hand over a candle, throw your attendant body from a window! Cut yourself. Fuck someone. *Feel*!

Calmer actuarial minds are advising that people sell minor experiences they can live without in order to purchase what server space they can. Cradle89 Bank is on hand to make those transactions.

Someone near me murmurs, "Well what if we're not one of the selected Cradles? And you go and sell all your experiences? Is this just a grab for experiences by those who've gotten bored with everything they have?"

Once, a few years ago, there was a trend among barge-dwellers and some Master Bodies to buy mundane, low-status experiences. I could've made some money selling things like washing an old car in a driveway, or making pancakes on a Sunday morning, or cleaning a toilet. Taking a city bus. Riding a bike on a boardwalk. Staying in a mildewy motel. Picnicking in a park.

I think about what I could give up to get some space now. My collection of bequeathed experiences is odd. Maybe I can do without some of them. I've got lots of cold-weather stuff, for example. My family spent some time in Quadrant 3, what was once called the mid-Atlantic, and my grandma Sarah liked the cold. So I've got things like crawling into deep snow tunnels, being hit in the face with packed snowballs, slipping and sliding and skating on ice, even falling. I've got cheeks pressed against cold, foggy windows. Warm breath on stiff, cold fingers. I'm not sure how much any of these are worth.

It's true most people who could afford lush Smooth World lives, but not access to the *entire* world, went for warmer climes. They purchased packaged simulacra of Southern Europe or Mexico or the Pacific Islands. But maybe they're getting bored with that now. Maybe they'll want to play middle class, middle of winter, mid-Atlantic. You never know. Maybe my odder family experiences can be sold as a kind of *It's a Wonderful Life* scenario. We've all watched that Precious Ancient Document, or PAD, a lot. They were poor, but there was snow, and Christmas ornaments.

My family was clearly odd, though. Seriously, they copyrighted falling on ice? But there can't be that many copyrighted cold, wet-weather sensations out there. Maybe there's a market for them?

"What're you gonna do?" Alex asks, interrupting my frantic thoughts. And I realize she's interlaced her hand with mine and she's rubbing my palm with her thumb. It's the most exquisite thing I've ever felt. So I scoot closer to her so our thighs are touching. I bring my other hand around hers. It feels like—it *is*—the end of the world, and everyone's inhibitions are falling. We're sitting in a plastic, putty-colored corridor, our backs against a warm wall.

Life in the Cradle hasn't been as drab as it might at first seem to someone coming from the sensorial past. We've had our celebrations, our friendships. We've had stories, imaginations, hobby groups, exercise classes. PAD nights were always fun, everyone watching together, passing around tequila, couples stealing off into the corners to make out. It was an unspoken rule that the authorities would usually look the other way as long as no one was doing anything that could lead to procreation. Oh, how I wish I'd had the courage to do something, anything, with Alex. Now we're out of time.

"I don't know," I say. "I could maybe sell some stuff…" I trace the ridges of her knuckles.

I know Alex actually has some space. She was describing to me one time the packages she'd purchased and the experiences she was going to implement. The dog, of course. And some kind of vehicle without a top, too. She's planning on driving across the desert, her black hair streaming out behind her, the dog by her side, some music on the cassette player, whatever that is. She wants to just keep moving and moving until she runs out of steam, so she purchased a bunch of travel-experience packages at great expense. She hopes she can make it to another continent, at least, before her body gives out.

A terrible thought occurs to me. "The Master Bodies," I blurt out.

"What?"

"We don't have any here."

I was told that my Master Body resides somewhere in Quadrant 42, near what was once called Denver, Colorado. Only some of the Cradles support them because they take up a lot of space, all lined up in their sensory-deprivation units, patched in to the Smooth World permanently, and needled and tubed up for bodily functions and food, tended for cleaning and turning.

I follow this terrible thought to its end. "Wouldn't they be more likely to keep the Cradles that have Master Bodies? We don't have any. Do you know how many Cradles don't have any?"

I'm trying to calculate the chances that we're gonna be mothballed. Lots of other people are going crazy like this too. There are too many questions.

The Supreme Leader was light on details, and you can tell the Cradle authorities were caught off guard. They don't know how it's gonna work. All they can tell people is, if you've got nowhere to go at the appointed time—be it into your own personal Smooth World or back into attendance—you're screwed. There will be no more latching in after the Cradle AI goes on austerity mode. There'll be no more protein pill shipments, no water purification, no air conditioning, no tequila, no lights, no moisture for the greenhouses. You'll be in a tomb.

"Leia, you have to try to get some space," Alex says. "Unless you just want to latch in and serve for what remains of your life." She stands and pulls me up with her.

I've stopped calculating. I'm just feeling her warm palm and being pulled through the corridor, back out into the canteen, across the other activity spaces, into one of the far corridors. She tugs me toward the line for Quadrant89 Bank. It's long, though. Very long. People hunker against each other, eyes peering around. They look at the clocks on the wall, wondering if there's time.

The crazies are mumbling about a scam. Maybe there's actually no more server space. Maybe they're just buying up your life's remaining experiences for worthless money. Maybe, since everyone in the country is now selling their experiences, they're worth less than nothing. It's one of those manufactured crises.

We stand at the end of the line, arms wrapped around each other. At 22:15, we still can't see the door of the bank.

"Alex," I say. "Forget it. It's not worth it."

"Huh? Leia…"

"Come on." I pull her out of line and back out across the space. It's starting to empty. Everyone's taking what they have and heading to their pods, and you can't tell by looking at them whether they're heading toward their own modest—or even luxurious—Smooth Worlds, or back into service for the Master Bodies.

Either way, it's eventual starvation, whether you do it in some bacchanalian free-for-all of your own creation, in a basic package that has you sitting in a deck chair with some sort of view, or in a stuffy, gothic bedroom, getting up occasionally to pour tea or dress your Master Body for dinner.

I start to run, tugging her. We stumble into the green-house, and I make for a corner behind the fruit trees.

DENNY'S MANNING TWO or three monitors, shooting around in his chair. His fingers are flying. Time: 22:45. He's murmuring an oldie, "It's the end of the world as we *know* it… and I feel fine."

"Donuts this time… maybe. Can you do donuts? We need a taste that'll knock her socks off. Chocolate glazed. With that sugar that melts in your mouth. She's never had donuts… that I know of."

"I can do anything, love."

"And be sure to stick in a distraction. That fool body can't remember what it purchased at this point. Give it something good, something obscene. I don't want it freezing any of her functions this time just for fun. And the AI—"

"Workin' on it, babe," Denny says and runs a harried hand through his thin hair. Then he mumbles, "Take that, you jealous beast," as he hacks into the cradle AI and freezes its ability to put stops on anyone's attendant functions. It'll alert the authorities, but by the time anyone can get suited up and in a rover, it'll all be over anyway.

"Right," Annie whispers. "Leia's set up. Shall we expand the revolution?"

✦ ✦ ✦

MY BODY'S HUMMING. We're still kissing. My hand rests between her warm legs. She's smiling. She has her hand on my stomach and then we're just still, holding each other. The fingers of my other hand are plunged into the soil of the small orchard.

An old thought jags into my brain. "Why this?"

"This? Oh, not this topic again." She laughs a ghost of a laugh.

"No seriously, why'd we spend money on this? Even if we couldn't stop what was happening, we could've invested in space travel, space living. We could all be boarding rockets now, or shuttles, or whatever. We might have begun populating a whole other planet by now. We could have ice planets. Even death stars would be better. What a fucking waste."

There's silence as the irrigation sprinklers shut off. I close my eyes and hear dripping, and Alex's heart beating. That's all.

"Leia," she says softly. "It's time."

"I know."

TIME: 24:17. I can't latch back out. So that's it, then. We were mothballed. Dead. I'm in service for the rest of my life, what remains of it. I can't remember what my last meal was or when. How long will my body hold out?

I stand and regard the Master Body with that odd combination of loyalty and envy. It's still there, so I guess Quadrant 42's Cradle is still up and running. It's on its bed of course, involved in a ridiculous, unattractive orgy. Bodies of all different shapes and unnatural hues are writhing about, emitting urgent sounds. One of the Lithe Things splits open, and its companions grab off chunks of it and eat it, chocolate- and vanilla-scented gunk running out over their chins.

I'm going to spend the rest of my life in here, I think distantly. *Might as well find something to do to distract myself for a while.*

I look away toward a little table by the window. There's the same chunky sandwich again, emitting those amazing scents. But there's also a little plate piled with something else, I see. I glance at the Master Body and then walk to the table. No one stops me.

On the plate are little flaky circular things with something that looks like chocolate draped over them. I think, *Donuts.* I think these were called donuts. I've seen lots of PADs with them. It was often police officers munching them in the front

seats of their patrol cars, cups of coffee balanced on dash-
boards. Had the Master Body ordered food again? Would I
dare, at the end of the world, steal a bite?

With my attendant hand, I pull the heavy drapes aside to
look out the window instead. I haven't bothered since the time
I looked through this window with these eyes and all there was
was another room—white, shiny, sterile, piled high with
something that looked like how money *used* to look, little
dusty-green stacks of paper.

But this time... stars. Thick twists of them spilling out
across a blue-black sky. A mountain is silhouetted against
these twists and spills. My mountain. My grandfather's
mountain.

"Huh," I say and idly allow the attendant hand to pick up
one of the donuts and the attendant mouth to bite into it. Why
not?

Instantly, these knees actually buckle. The knees of the
middle-aged Smooth World attendant body in the maid's
uniform with the tiny white apron give way. I have to throw a
hand out and catch the table to keep from falling. Some kind
of fierce white light rims everything in sight, the edges of the
window frame, the curtains. The inside of this mouth sparks
and waters, dribbling saliva. The stomach contracts happily,
and something down below it even comes alive too. I can feel
glittering things in the fingertips. My fingertips?

I think of Alex. I think of the sugary, full feeling of coming with her. Tears roll down these soft cheeks. The glass of the big window pulses and clouds faintly, like there's real air on the other side. I hold up a hand but there's no heat. I unlatch the window and it swings easily open, creaking.

Cool air rushes in, carrying a hundred unfamiliar scents. These ears hear a rustling, perhaps the branches of a small stand of trees these eyes can see just outside the window.

This body panics. It looks back over its shoulder, thinking the Master Body must be on to it now, but there's nothing there but more black air, a sky full of more stars, another mountain. I turn the torso again, and there's no more window even.

"We're not in Kansas anymore, Toto," I whisper with these lips—my lips?—thinking of one of my favorite PADs. In fact, watching it on a TV in an old, musty motel room and eating popcorn and sipping Coke is one of my family's experiential properties.

There is nothing to do but walk toward the mountain. Out there, out at the far edge of the desert that is no longer a field of solar panels, but instead small stands of delicate, spindly yellow-green trees and low brush, rocks. And I can see a long, lighted streak snaking by. A train, I believe. Something once called a train. I can hear a far-off bell, a faint rumbling as of steel on clickity-clack tracks. I'll head there.

Maybe Alex will be on that train. Maybe not.

The Argo Affair

by Lisa Timpf

GINA ROSE CHECKED her wrist chrono. *Four hours to go in the shift.* Suppressing a yawn, she frowned as K-9 patrol dog Buddy stopped abruptly, blocking her forward progress. The German shepherd peered down a laneway threading the gap between two tall buildings. Buddy's triangular ears flicked forward, and he whined deep in his throat.

Gina jerked her head toward the laneway, and her patrol partner, Jim Spenser, nodded in reply. The two officers sidestepped into the narrow, semi-dark alley, stun-guns drawn, the dog preceding them.

The low rumble of a garb-grinder grew louder as they inched forward. Back in 2116, the city councillors had passed a bylaw prohibiting grinders in the tonier parts of town. Here on the wrong side of the hop-train tracks, the grinders continued to serve a purpose, shredding and sorting garbage, then compressing the usable parts into fuel bricks for flex-feed furnaces.

When they'd approached within fifty feet of the device,

Buddy barked twice and raced forward. Seconds later, Gina heard an engine roar to life, and a blast of air sent her reeling backward as a hover bike sped out of the alley.

"Stop! Police!" Gina yelled. The bike's power-plant screamed louder in reply, and the black-clad driver crouched low over the vehicle's steering apparatus. Gina scowled into the darkness in the direction the bike had disappeared, swearing under her breath.

When Gina returned her attention to the laneway, she saw Jim frowning at a black vinyl luggage carrier in front of the garb-grinder's feeder door. The bag looked to be roughly six feet in length—the sort of thing favored by tourists packing hockey sticks or other unwieldy items.

"Would've been a trick to balance this on the bike," Jim mused, lifting the bag to peer under it. "Ah, I see. It's equipped with a hover feature—low-end model, mind you—and a tow rope."

"Quiet night," Gina commented. "Not many cameras in this neighborhood. It *could* have been towed, especially over a short distance."

She slipped a neoprene glove onto her right hand to avoid disturbing evidence, then undid the bag's zipper.

Jim trained his flashlight into the opening. Gina drew in her breath as she glimpsed a wan face. She dropped to her knees, checked for a pulse, then quickly withdrew her hand. She clenched her jaw muscles, then reached in again.

"What is it?" Jim asked.

"His neck. It's—all wrong." Gina didn't know how else to describe what she'd felt beneath the cream-colored silk scarf. There were slashes in the skin, almost like—"It feels like he has gills," she said. She continued to search for a pulse, knowing by the coldness of the skin that she wouldn't find it.

MOIRA JENKINS DREW her power wheelchair into place in front of her desk. She toggled her persacomp to life and started to sift through her Kwikmail.

Catching motion in her peripheral vision, Moira looked at her boss's glass-walled office as Captain Gilbert Daniels stood up and made his way to the door, followed by another man. The indigo-haired captain stood six feet, but the fellow beside him towered a good four inches taller. Moira studied the newcomer, trying to place him. She'd seen him around the precinct—new recruit, maybe, though he didn't carry himself like a raw kid just out of police college.

"Moira, I'd like you to meet Oskar Klein," Captain Gil said as he and the tall man stopped in front of Moira's desk.

"How do you do, Mr. Klein?" Moira said. He nodded in reply, his blue-gray eyes cryptic.

"Oskar just transferred to New Toronto from the Berlin Police Force," the captain said. "He finished his orientation with the department yesterday, and is ready for assignment.

He'll take Williamson's spot."

Moira nodded. With Williamson's retirement, she'd been wondering about a new partner.

"You can set up here." Moira gestured to the brand-new state-of-the-art workstation opposite her own worn faux-wood desk. "By the way, this's Nikuru Akai, our assistant—he goes by Akai." Moira gestured toward the short, lean man seated to her left. "He's an analyst, but that doesn't do his talents justice." She shot Akai a teasing grin, and he waved his hand dismissively in response. "We call him the computer whisperer."

Captain Daniels cleared his throat. "We have a case for you three to work. Night shift found a body in an alley just off Seymour Street last night." He nodded in Moira's direction. "Why don't you show Oskar the way to the Medical Examiner's lab? The body's there now."

"Sure thing," Moira said, rolling her chair back from the desk with a flip of the arm-mounted controls. "Follow me."

"I DON'T KNOW what it is about midnight shift," Medical Examiner Lachlan Reid grumbled. "They seem to bring in the oddest cases." Lachlan gestured toward the body laid on the stainless-steel table. "Webbed fingers." He lifted the victim's right hand so Moira and Oskar could see the membrane of pink skin joining the digits. "Webbed feet, too. Gills on the neck. Dorsal fin on the back."

"Is he human, or—" Moira asked.

"He's Earth stock, alright, with some bio-mods, plastic surgery, and implants mostly. Pretty slick, too—whoever did them, did a good job." Lachlan's voice conveyed grudging admiration.

"Do you have a cause of death?" Moira asked.

"Gunshot wound," Lachlan said. "From close range. His heart's in the normal place, at least. Shooter knew that."

"Time of death?"

"About 2:30 a.m., give or take fifteen minutes."

Oskar moved closer to the table. He sniffed, then raised his eyebrows.

"You noticed it, did you?" Lachlan grunted. "He's absorbed a chemical into his skin. That accounts for the spicy smell. Not likely the result of diet—I'm thinking something he was exposed to." He leaned forward, the gleam in his eyes betraying his pleasure in showing off superior knowledge. "Rhysantine."

"Never heard of it," Moira confessed.

"I have," Oskar said. "I read an article about that new planet the Galactic Expeditionary Forces discovered last year."

"Argo," Lachlan said, nodding. "Rhysantine is a compound they found in the ocean water. The question is, what's it doing on this guy?"

✦ ✦ ✦

MOIRA AND OSKAR exited the elevator and headed to their work area. She smiled. If she was reading his body language right, Akai felt pleased with himself. Which must mean—

"I was able to confirm the identity of the deceased, based on the intake photos," Akai said as he connected his persacomp to the view-board. "Logan Roberts, age 24." The image of a man with brush-cut brown hair and deep brown eyes appeared on the board. "His most recent place of work is listed as Gen-Alpha."

Moira's eyes narrowed. "Aren't they under contract with the North American Colonization Service?"

"Yes." Akai posted an image of a large, two-floor, white stucco building with several windows along the front. He tipped his head toward the screen. "Gen-Alpha's office is located just north of New Toronto."

"Did Mr. Roberts have any family?" Oskar asked.

"A sister, Evie Roberts," Akai replied. "She's younger, just 22." An image of a woman with shoulder-length brown hair and deep brown eyes flashed on the screen. "Both parents were killed in a car accident when Logan was 16. Evie works as a robot tech at the Powervac facility in Scarborough."

"Thanks, Akai," Moira said. She looked at Oskar. "First stop, Gen-Alpha HQ. Sound good?" She waited for Oskar's nod before turning to face the analyst. "Akai, if you can do the usual background checks, including financial, that would be great."

Moira scooted her wheelchair back from her desk and bee-lined for the elevator with Oskar striding behind her.

"Not my business to pry, but are you feeling alright?" Oskar asked as Moira steered with the specially-outfitted SUV's hand controls.

"I'm fine," Moira said, stifling a yawn. "I didn't sleep well," she added more softly. *Three weeks till the deadline to decide whether to sign on for another five years of service. Why I put it off I don't know...* But she knew, deep down inside, why she'd done so. Solving crimes wasn't the same anymore, without her mentor Williamson. And while her sister Sophie's invitation to try her hand at coaching, helping out with the Vancouver Spirit Bears women's hockey team, had tempted her initially, she didn't feel the same about the sport since her career-ending injury. Which left her without a lot of options.

With an effort, Moira brought her attention back to the here-and-now.

"GPS says to turn left just ahead," Oskar said, pointing with his left arm.

"Ah, I see it now," Moira said as the Gen-Alpha headquarters came into view. It was recognizable from the image Akai had shown.

When they arrived at the building, the glass entry doors slid open with a hiss. The sunlight flowing in through the skylights made the reception area bright and airy.

A man who had been standing off to the side of the reception desk came forward. Clad in dark-gray pinstriped slacks and a black bomber-style jacket over a snow-white polo shirt, he might have stepped from the pages of a men's fashion magazine. "Elias J. Huber, Gen-Alpha CEO," he said in a hearty voice, extending his hand to each of the detectives in turn. He smiled, showing dazzlingly white, even teeth. "Your message wasn't specific. How may I help you?"

"If there's somewhere private we might talk..." Moira suggested, quirking her eyebrows upward.

"Of course." Elias led the way to a conference room, closing the sturdy beige door behind them. On the far wall, a photo frame projected a rolling series of breathtakingly beautiful images—yellow skies over brooding magenta mountains, a forest of towering purple-leaved trees, green oceans with surging waves. Moira recognized the ocean shot as an image of the planet Arcadia, currently being settled with colonists drawn primarily from North America's East Coast.

In the center of the room, an oblong maple-wood table provided a discussion space. Moving smoothly but without fuss, Elias pulled one of the seats to the side to create a gap for Moira's powerchair.

"Logan Roberts is one of your employees, I believe?" Moira

asked once everyone had settled into place.

"Yes. I know Logan well." Elias frowned. "He didn't report for the pool session this morning. Biometrics indicate he's still in his room. It's not unusual, given the stressors placed on them, for our employees to need extra sleep to recharge their batteries."

"Why the biometrics?" Oskar asked.

"We monitor our gen-mod employees' vitals overnight," Elias explained. "We had some incidents early on with adverse reactions to the alterations. When readings fall outside pre-set parameters, an auto-alarm triggers."

"We'd like a copy of the bio-readouts for last night, for all participants," Moira said briskly.

"I'll arrange that," Elias replied.

"Back to Logan. I'm afraid we have bad news. Patrol found him dead just after 3 a.m., in an alley off Seymour Street," Moira said. She studied Elias' face.

"Dead?" Elias rubbed his eyes with the heels of his palms. He sighed. "With the Trials five days away, I was afraid something like this might happen."

"Trials?" Oskar asked.

"Do you know anything about Gen-Alpha and what we do?" Elias straightened in his chair. Seeing his guests' expressions, he nodded. "Makes sense. After all, our work *is* supposed to be secret."

He paused, as though considering where to begin. "I'll give

you the short version. You know that as new planets that are potentially habitable are found, the Galactic Alliance opens them up for colonization proposals from member species?"

"I'm not familiar with the details," Moira said.

"The number of proposals accepted depends on the planet—resources, availability of suitable settlement sites, and so on." Elias paused. "Our role is to develop bid packages on behalf of the North American Colonization Service. We won the first planet, Arcadia, but lost out on the next two because other species were deemed more adaptable and therefore more likely to experience success. After our second setback, the Colonization Service agreed to what we've proposed all along."

"Which is?" Oskar's brow furrowed.

"Biological modification. Not everyone. Just a certain number of genetically-modified colonists with specialized attributes allotted to each settlement. If the mods seem beneficial long-term, we can adjust DNA so they become hereditary. Of course, smaller genetic tweaks such as adaptations to eye function for a brighter or much dimmer planet can be done for all."

"The fins, the gills, the webbed feet and hands... Logan's role was to assist with the colonization of Argo," Moira speculated.

"Exactly." Huber nodded. "Each prospective settlement world requires its own mods. Ludwiks Planet, for example, is mostly woodland, and the trees are massive." He gestured toward the photo frame, which currently displayed the purple-leaved forest. "We've equipped seven of the prospective colonists with prototype wings, which they're just starting to master. From all accounts, flight is an exhilarating experience."

"You mentioned an event in five days," Moira prompted.

"Yes. That's when the settlement bids for Argo will be presented. The bid process requires each team to navigate test scenarios based on the planet's features. It's Earth's turn to host. Otherwise we'd be on our way already." His expression darkened. "If someone wanted to undermine our proposal, this could be the first step. It's important we find out as soon as possible who's behind this."

"Who might want to harm Gen-Alpha or interfere with the bid?" Moira asked.

"I wish I could say I couldn't think of anyone," Huber answered, unable to repress a bark of sarcastic laughter. "But there are plenty of folks who don't support us. The KHH—Keep Humans Human—protesters, for example—they've been giving us grief lately, though how they found out about the operation—" he shrugged. "Then, there are the other species competing for the same planet—the Formosa and the G'nava aren't above sabotage. Neither one of them have any known emissaries on Earth at present. Once you find the killer, though, it's possible they had a hand in it, long-distance."

"Any internal squabbles?" asked Oskar. "Anyone who might want Logan dead?"

"When you work this closely with the same people day after day, under intense conditions, you get flare-ups. Logan seemed to be a lightning rod," Elias said, tapping his fingers against the tabletop. "Whether that led to murder—hard to believe. Our psych checks are rigorous, and with ongoing monitoring we ought to have weeded out anyone who would let a personal conflict escalate to that level. Still, it's possible," he conceded.

"We'll need to interview Logan's teammates, anyone who had contact with him," Moira said.

"Of course," Elias replied, rising to his feet. "I'll hook you up with our Human Resources manager, Alina."

As if on cue, an auburn-haired woman with a pleasant expression entered the room.

After exchanging greetings with Alina, Oskar rose and moved toward the door. Elias raised a hand to deter Moira's exit, and she halted her powerchair.

"If I may have a moment of your time…" Elias said, darting a glance toward the now-closed portal through which Oskar had already passed. "This may seem forward… If so, forgive me. But I wanted to mention that we're still looking for recruits for our team on Ludwiks Planet. The flight-enabled squad is responsible for both security and exploration, and I don't have a suitable leader for that group yet. Before you came here today, I had you short-listed as one of the people I wanted to meet with." He handed her a jumpchip with his contact information. "If you decide that's of interest to you…"

"I'm almost fifty-five years old," Moira protested. "In the Forces, that's pushing it."

"Yes," Elias said. "But the human life span now averages, what… 140, 150? You're old enough to have valuable experience, young enough to give us value for some time. And I'm aware that your current contract is almost up."

"Flight—" she said, rolling the word off her tongue. "How?"

Elias, eyes gleaming with enthusiasm, spread his arms. "Wing attachments—computer-controlled, very sophisticated. Not biomods, although we do need to make some adjustments to the users' bodies."

Moira closed her eyes for a moment, imagining the exhilaration of soaring above the tops of those massive trees. *Steady,* she told herself. *You have a job to do.*

"I'll need time to consider it," she said. "Right now, my focus is this case. After that… Thank you for the information."

With a nod, she steered her powerchair out of the room. Speeding down the ice had sometimes felt like flying, but this—this would be… She shook her head. *The case. Focus on the case.*

"I'LL START BY showing you the workout area," Alina said as she led the way through a maze of hallways. "Ah, here we are."

She opened the door to reveal a large, rectangular room with a view-board at one end. Along the wall opposite the door, a low-silled window overlooked the pool.

"That's the Argo team down there," Alina said, pointing with her chin. Moira wheeled over to the window and peered down while Oskar took up a position to her right.

Five male swimmers splashed down their respective lanes in the blue-green water, dorsal fins arching upward.

"Right now, the team's performing their morning drills. Every fifth day, they use a racing format. Many of the prospective colonists are former competitive athletes. The races keep them sharp," Alina explained.

"Speaking of competitiveness," Moira asked, her face thoughtful, "is there a chance someone might have wanted Logan out of the way to better their own position in the colony?"

"Not likely," Alina replied. "All of our candidates, if our bid is successful, will be deployed. As for the Trials, we carry ten people, with two spares. Based on demerits he'd accumulated, Logan was already slotted to be one of the extras. There'd be no advantage to other team members to harm him."

Moira watched as the swimmers picked up the pace coming back toward the starting blocks. The first to touch the wall popped upright, shaking his white hair to release a spray of water. Seconds later, the others reached the end point. Though she couldn't hear any words exchanged, Moira could tell from the body language that the swimmers were now engaged in playful banter as they lifted themselves, arm muscles bulging, out of the water and onto the pool deck. Six female swimmers took positions on the blocks. The white-haired male swimmer who'd touched the wall first in the men's race counted down the time, and the women dove into the pool and started churning the water as they headed for the far end.

Moira sighed. The group below radiated health and high spirits. The news she and Oskar bore would undoubtedly shatter the mood. Logan's death could well cast a pall over the team, resulting in diminished performance at the upcoming event. Maybe that was the intention.

"You have other groups preparing for trials as well, right?" Moira asked.

"Yes," Alina replied. "Two other teams, slated to represent us in the competitions for other planets. However, there's not much interaction between the squads. Logan spent the majority of his time with the Argo group."

Moira nodded. They'd start with the Argo team, and with any employees performing central functions that interfaced with all the groups.

+   +   +

"KARINA CHOWNYK, RIGHT?" Moira beamed a tight smile at the stern-faced young woman seated in front of her. She clicked on the voice recorder, as protocol demanded. "What's your role with Gen-Alpha?"

"I'm a psych-tech," Karina replied. "My role is to monitor the emotional and psychological well-being of the colonists."

"It's an unusual setting. Lot of pressures," Oskar commented.

"Some of the team members struggle with the biological adaptations, to start with," Karina replied. "It's one thing in theory, but when it really happens... There's also the request to stay on the Gen-Alpha campus, to keep the project low-profile. Some find that isolating."

"Is it mandatory, staying on campus?" Moira asked, her tone crisp.

"No," Karina replied. "But colonists are asked to limit their exposure to the outside world, and when they do go off-campus, to conceal the more obvious physical changes. Fortunately, with our location so close to the Malton Space-port, people often just assume they're from off-planet if they get spotted."

"Was Logan one of those who spent time off-campus?" Moira asked.

"Yes," Karina said, as though she regretted having to divulge this information.

"Did others resent that, maybe see his actions as jeopardizing the project?" Moira prodded.

"I can guess where you're going with this." Karina squared

her shoulders. "We vet our people very carefully. They complete a barrage of psych tests before acceptance into the program. I don't believe any of our staff are capable of murder, particularly over breaking the rules."

"Yet someone killed Logan Roberts," Moira said, her voice soft. "It's our job to find out who."

SEVERAL INTERVIEWS LATER, Moira didn't feel she was any further ahead.

One more to go, she told herself. "Rutger Milvery?" Moira asked, checking the name on the roster Alina had provided.

The short, broad-shouldered man seated across the conference table nodded curtly, his emerald-green eyes guarded. Though he appeared to be the same age as Logan, his pure-white hair lent an aura of greater maturity.

"I'm not sure if you'd heard, but we're here investigating the murder of one of your coworkers, Logan Roberts," Moira said gently.

Rutger raised and lowered his left shoulder.

"How did you get along with Logan?" Moira asked.

"To be honest," he replied, "I didn't hang out with him outside of work, and tried to avoid him on the job. The guy was a jerk. Arrogant, self-centered. In the last six months, he'd started showing up late, and honestly didn't seem to be that into it."

"Do you know anyone who might want to harm him?" Moira asked.

"No one in here would take that step," Rutger said decisively.

"We've asked this of all those we interviewed, so don't take this personally," Moira said, smiling. "Where were you between one and four a.m. Wednesday morning?"

"Asleep," Rutger replied, leaning back with his arms crossed. "You can check my biostats if you need proof."

Once she'd indicated to Rutger he was free to go, Moira stretched her arms and rolled her shoulders.

"His story fell in line with the others." Oskar drummed his fingers on the table. "As to the biostats, if Logan's could be circumvented, there's no reason to think others couldn't be as well. What next, back to the precinct?"

Before Moira could respond, her comm device buzzed. "Akai," she said, after scanning through the text message. "He sent Evie's address."

"The sister?" Oskar asked as he rose from the table. Seeing Moira's affirming nod, he turned and headed for the door. "Let's go."

MOIRA STUDIED THE young woman sitting at the fold-down table. With her brown hair and eyes, long nose, and broad mouth, Evie Roberts bore an undeniable resemblance to the deceased.

Evie clearly had started to cope with her brother's loss. She'd greeted them calmly at the door of her cramped but tidy apartment. The line of questioning they needed to take would be like ripping a Band-Aid off a fresh wound. Still, it had to be done. The more quickly they unearthed information, the better their chances of solving the case. Best to plunge ahead.

"Was your brother in trouble of any sort?" Moira asked.

"Trouble? I don't know about that," Evie answered. "I know he wasn't particularly happy."

"Can you elaborate on that?"

"In high school, he was an all-around athlete," Evie replied. "Good in a number of sports. He swam on the varsity team at University of New Toronto. Logan made it to the national trials in the butterfly and freestyle events, but just missed out on an Olympic berth. He'd hoped to win big, score some endorsements. When that didn't come through, he took it hard. Then he landed the job at Gen-Alpha."

"So you knew about Gen-Alpha?" Oskar jumped in.

Evie nodded. "He insisted on coming to visit me and dressed in such a way that you couldn't see his—his—" Her hands fluttered around her neck.

"We know," Moira replied. She paused, considering how to word her next question. "We gathered from talking to people at his workplace that there were some conflicts with coworkers. Did he ever talk about that?"

"Some of them got on his case." Evie's voice sounded stronger now, almost defiant. "He was a good brother, a good guy. They didn't understand—"

"Didn't understand what?" Oskar asked, leaning forward.

"He worked more than one job," Evie answered. She covered her face with her hands and rocked back and forth. "It's my fault. My loan. I didn't know—" Struggling to maintain composure, Evie looked up to face the officers. "When I took my degree at UNT, I couldn't get a bank loan, so I borrowed money from a place up the street. They looked legit, but I found out later that they were tied to the Front Street Syndicate."

"And when they wanted their money back, I'll bet they weren't too patient," Moira said.

"They made threats." Evie glanced down at her hands. "I didn't tell Logan at first. But he knew something was wrong. He wanted to help."

"Anyone else you would suggest we talk to, to understand what was going on?" Oskar asked.

"He had a girlfriend, I think," Evie said slowly. "Karina. She worked at Gen-Alpha, too."

Moira and Oskar exchanged glances. "She neglected to mention that," Moira said.

"The company has a policy against fraternization." Evie put her hand over her mouth. "I probably shouldn't have told you."

"This is a murder investigation," Oskar replied. "You *need* to tell us everything you know."

"That's it. I *have* told you everything," Evie said, rising from the table.

After they left the building, Moira stopped her wheelchair and looked up at Oskar.

"When she answered those last few questions, her posture seemed guarded. Think she told us the whole truth?" Moira asked.

"I don't think she lied." Oskar's voice sounded solemn. "But she may have left something out."

"Agreed." Moira resumed her forward progress. "If we need to, we'll circle back to her. Meanwhile, I'd like to hear what Karina has to say for herself."

✦   ✦   ✦

KARINA CHOWNYK SAT in the Gen-Alpha conference room, scowling at the two detectives. "What more can I tell you?" she asked, raising her hands palms-upward.

"You didn't mention you were dating the victim," Moira replied, narrowing her eyes.

Karina bowed her head. "If they find out, I could lose my job." Her voice contained a hint of pleading.

"We aren't planning to tattle," Moira said, keeping her voice firm. "However, being less than forthright with us a second time might test our patience."

"Fine," Karina sighed, fiddling with her shoulder-length hair. "We dated." She frowned. "When he was available."

"Meaning?" Oskar asked.

"He always had something on the go, you know?" Karina's eyes blazed. "That sister of his, and her loan—he was helping her pay it off, so he took jobs on the side."

"What kind of jobs?" Moira asked.

"He wouldn't tell me." Karina looked down at the table. "That caused a lot of friction between us. In fact, I gave serious thought to breaking it off."

"Why didn't you?" Oskar asked.

"Because,"—Karina met Oskar's gaze and offered a rare smile—"despite what his coworkers might tell you, Logan was a sweetheart, deep down, with a great sense of humor. We had a lot of fun. I really did care for him."

"ANYTHING COME OUT of the search of the victim's dorm unit yesterday?" Moira asked as she positioned her powerchair in front of her desk the next morning. *It's the best I've felt in weeks,* she reflected as she sipped on her coffee. Instead of obsessing over whether to retire or lock in for another five years, she'd dreamed of flying.

"Looked like someone had beat us to it," Akai replied. "As we pulled in, we saw a dark SUV squealing out of the parking lot." The analyst leaned forward. "Logan wasn't the best housekeeper. The shelves and furniture were covered in dust, which turned out to be a break for us. We saw a rectangular clean spot where someone must have removed an item. I'm guessing it's one of those projection frames where you can plug in a jump-chip and display photos."

"Anything else?" Moira asked.

"Whoever got there first threw some papers around, and several pieces of furniture looked out of place. A coffee table tipped over, things like that. It looked like we didn't get there too much later than the person we chased off." Akai's eyes glinted. "Our search clarified why I didn't find anything suspicious on Logan's financials. He had a stash of credit coins—some of them marked."

"Marked?"

"Gangs unit put a sting operation on the Front Street Syndicate a week back," Akai explained. "The ID on the coins in Logan's room match."

Oskar settled back in his chair, his face thoughtful. "So, our friend may have had some affiliation with a gang. Maybe *that* was his second job."

"Good work," Moira said to Akai. "Oskar and I need to catch up with our undercover operative in the Front Street Syndicate, see what she knows."

✦   ✦   ✦

RYOTA KANEKO SCANNED her surroundings uneasily as she

fidgeted on the wooden bench. Moira and Oskar stood nearby, apparently deep in conversation with one another.

"Make it quick," Ryota muttered nervously. The hands-free device she wore enabled her to speak to the nearby officers without arousing suspicion. She looked like any number of the people around them who engaged in animated conversations on their comm units as they enjoyed the park.

"Did a guy named Logan Roberts ever work for the Front Street gang?" Moira asked.

Ryota's brow wrinkled. "Doesn't ring a bell. What's he look like?"

"Dark brown hair, brush cut, long nose." Moira paused, then added, "Webbed fingers, gills, dorsal fin."

"Oh, Big Fish," Ryota said. "Yeah, he did some work stealing stuff from private yachts, making pickups at drop points in the water, that sort of thing. Why?"

"He turned up dead," Moira said. "Think the Syndicate would off him?"

"Rumor has it he didn't bring in as much money as he should have on his last score," Ryota replied. "They might have thought he was pulling a fast one." She scanned the park, scowled at something in the distance, and rose to her feet in a smooth motion. "Gotta go. Hey, you might want to check out one thing," she said as she shouldered her jacket into position. "Big Fish liked to pound back the brews at the Flying Warthog. Liam Branders runs the place. Might know something."

"We'll check that out, thanks," Moira said. "We have another stop to make first."

"THIS IS THE address," Oskar said, looking at the red-brick semi-detached house with the sagging porch. Then he glanced nervously at the porch steps and over at Moira.

Moira toggled a switch, sending her powerchair into hover mode. After piloting her way up the steps, she landed in front of the door. "The hover feature's handy, but it uses a lot of power, so I limit its use," she explained once Oskar had bounded up the steps to join her. She grinned. "You should see the look on criminals' faces when we get into a chase situation."

Oskar smiled as he knocked on the door. The portal creaked open and a man with a faded scar across his left cheek appeared in the entryway.

"Harold Gray?" Moira asked as she displayed her badge. "We'd like to talk to you."

The man put a hand up to sweep away a shock of hair that hung over his eyes, peered at Moira's I.D., then opened the door wider. "I've got nothing to hide," he mumbled. "Follow me."

Harold led the way through a dimly-lit hallway into a cluttered kitchen. In the center of the room stood a table, a cheap, wobbly-looking affair accompanied by four chairs that looked equally suspect. On one of the chairs, a heap of leaflets printed on neon-green paper stood in an untidy stack. Moira had time to read the text: "Gen-Alpha Must Be Stopped!" before Harold scooped the pamphlets off the chair and tossed them onto the kitchen counter. He moved the chair aside to make space for her.

Oskar eased his tall frame onto the seat at the far end of the table, moving gingerly, with the air of someone expecting at any moment to hear the cracking of disintegrating wood.

"What's this about?" Harold asked, jutting his chin forward.

"A Gen-Alpha employee showed up dead," Moira replied, deciding not to pull any punches. "We're checking to see who might know something about it."

"Well, I don't," Harold snapped, folding his arms over his chest.

"You're no fan of Gen-Alpha," Oskar said, jutting his chin forward.

"Of course not." Harold spat the words out. "You start messing with humans the way they are and when do they stop being human? It's a fine line, one they have no right to walk."

"Where were you Wednesday morning between one and four a.m.?" Moira asked.

"On an overnight turbotrain, heading back from Vancouver," Harold replied. "I was at a conference. Stayed a couple of extra days to take in the sights."

"What about other members of your group? Anyone who might act on their own?" Oskar asked.

Harold shook his head. "We believe in the sanctity of human life," he replied. "That's why we're against what Gen-Alpha is doing. Who was the deceased?"

"Logan Roberts," Moira replied.

Harold's face blanched.

"What's wrong?" Oskar asked.

"We were supposed to meet this afternoon. He promised to show me evidence of Gen-Alpha's work. For a price, of course. He'd be the last person I'd want to harm."

"Why would he feed *you* information?" Moira asked.

"Money," Harold replied. "He didn't explain, but I had a feeling he really needed money."

"LIAM BRANDERS." THE Flying Warthog's proprietor, a tall, broad-shouldered man, grinned as he extended his hand across the bar's polished wood surface. "To what do I be owing the pleasure?"

Oskar flashed his badge. "We have a few questions."

Liam's expression turned sour. "I was hoping you were representatives from... never mind. Whatever it was, I didn't do it. I'm run off my feet day and night keeping the Flying Warthog going. Though if someone were to offer me enough money I'd sell this place in a minute and go back home to the

Independent Republic of Newfoundland."

"Is business that bad?" Moira asked.

Liam snorted. "Business is great. Booming. It's the customers that are the problem. Serving up a good pint of draft beer isn't good enough anymore. Everyone wants exotic drinks made from off-world ingredients. They're not cheap."

"We hear this guy is one of your regulars," Moira said, flashing up an image of Logan Roberts on her comm device.

Liam leaned forward and raised his bushy eyebrows. "Yep. Recognize him alright. He in trouble?"

"Suppose you could say so," Moira replied. "He's dead."

"Too bad," Liam commented. "Nice kid."

"You know anything that might help us understand who killed him, and why?" Oskar asked.

"Tuesday night, Logan seemed… different. More animated than usual. He talked about leaving town," Liam replied. "He'd had a few."

"You'd better tell us *everything* you know," Oskar said.

"Fine," Liam said, shoulders sagging. "I had word from the Front Street Syndicate that they wanted to know when Logan left the bar. It would be bad for business if I didn't tell them. So I made a call."

"That's interesting," Moira said. "Who'd you contact?"

"A guy named Eddie 'the Eel' Garcia." Liam rubbed his forehead, a rueful expression twisting his features. "If I'd known how it would end up—"

"Thanks," Moira said. Without a backward glance, she piloted the wheelchair out into the sunlight.

"You wrapped that up quickly," Oskar commented.

"We need to dispatch a search team to Eddie's place," Moira replied as she reached for her comm device. "Hopefully, they'll get there before Liam can warn him."

EDDIE GARCIA WAS no stranger to the interrogation room. Moira and Oskar let him cool his heels until the search results came back, but he showed no signs of agitation as he waited.

When the officers entered the room, Eddie looked up calmly. "Long time no see," he said to Moira. He ran his right hand through his poorly-trimmed sand-colored goatee as though trying to coax it into greater respectability.

Moira noticed Oskar's upward-arched eyebrows. "We went to high school together," she said, shrugging. She turned to face Garcia. "Hey, Eddie, what do you know about this guy?" Moira slammed a photo of Logan Roberts down on the table.

"We worked a couple of jobs together," Eddie said casually. "He had skills that came in handy." He smirked.

"Somebody killed him, Eddie." Moira's tone sharpened. "And rumor has it you had a tip-off as to his whereabouts Tuesday night. Or maybe I should say Wednesday morning."

"I got word from Liam, yeah. I high-tailed it to Logan's

place, just to chat." Eddie leaned back in his chair and shrugged. "Only, he never showed up. If somebody offed him, that explains why."

"Here's how I think it went down," Moira said. "You waited for Logan to come out of the Flying Warthog. When he did, you confronted him and shot him. You loaded him in an anti-grav transport bag and drove to the garb-grinder—conveniently located a mere five blocks away from the bar—and if you hadn't been interrupted, the body would have been gone."

"Why would I kill Logan Roberts?" Eddie protested.

"On the Syndicate's orders," Moira snapped. "They don't like to be double-crossed."

Eddie shook his head. "No way. Like I said, I wanted to talk to him, but he never showed."

"Maybe you can explain"—Oskar put another image down on the table, this time of a gun—"why the search team found this weapon stashed in your living room. No fingerprints, you're too smart for that, but Ballistics confirmed it's the gun that killed Logan Roberts."

"Never seen it before," Eddie said.

"Yeah, we get that a lot," Moira commented.

"No, seriously. Someone's trying to frame me."

"Why would they do that?" Moira asked, her eyes cold.

"Because they don't want you to know who really killed him," Eddie replied.

✦   ✦   ✦

MOIRA SIPPED ON her coffee, then slammed it on the table, almost sending a surge of hot liquid over the brim of her cup. "I know it looks bad for Garcia." She frowned, concentrating. "He's a small-time hood, and he's done a lot of things, but murder?"

"But the gun, and the request to keep tabs on Logan Roberts," Oskar said, as if in protest.

"He knows his way around hover bikes," Akai added. "A citation for drag racing is what brought him in here the last time." He fiddled with a 3-d holographic model showing the New Toronto neighborhood surrounding the Flying Warthog.

"The ME's report said the shooter fired from close range," Oskar said. "That suggests Logan knew his attacker. He *did* know Eddie."

"If Eddie was smart enough to wipe his prints off, why would he leave the gun in his apartment to be found?" Moira countered. "And if it was him, how did he get onto the campus to rummage through Logan's dorm unit?"

"I don't think he did," Akai said, pointing to the model. "Just finished checking street-cam footage between where Eddie was last spotted and the Flying Warthog."

"And?" Moira prompted.

"There's no way he could have gotten there in time to meet up with Logan. I don't see how he's our guy."

"If not him, who?" Oskar growled.

"We know it *wasn't* Harold Gray," Akai said. "His alibi checked out—rail company confirmed he was on the turbotrain." Akai's comm device buzzed, and he grunted as he read the message on the small screen. "Yesterday, patrol found a stolen hover bike stashed in an alley nine blocks away from where Gina and Jim found the body. The lab just finished its analysis of the bike. Said they found traces of rhysantine all over it."

Moira exchanged glances with Oskar. "It suggests that whoever piloted that bike was involved with the Gen-Alpha project," she said. "The candidates for the Argo trial all spent time in the pool. Alina told us it has the same chemical composition as Argo's ocean."

"Find anything from Logan's *Share-it* social-media profile?" Moira asked Akai.

"Not sure if it's relevant." Akai shrugged as he began flashing images on the viewboard. "I did get in to look around. I've narrowed down the photos to the ones I think might be important. I'll run through them now."

Moira focused intently as Akai projected images of Logan with his sister, some shots of birds and the ocean, and pictures from a Rappies basketball game Logan had attended.

"Wait," Moira said as Akai moved past an image from the game. "Back up."

Akai obliged.

Moira studied the photo of two men wearing scarves, with a neatly-dressed, serious-faced woman seated between them. "Notice anything?" she asked Oskar.

"Well, I'm guessing this might have been around the time Logan started dating Karina," Oskar replied.

"The third person, see the way he's looking at Karina?" she said softly.

"Yeah. I see," Oskar said.

"We need to go back to Gen-Alpha headquarters," Moira said, turning her powerchair to face the exit.

REALIZING THAT THEIR quarry might be less than enthused to see them, Oskar and Moira split up when they reached Gen-Alpha, with Oskar standing at the rear of the building while Moira took the front. If all went well, and Elias succeeded in shepherding their man into the conference room, he'd let them know. Instinct and years of experience told Moira the odds were against things going that smoothly. She tensed as she saw a flash of movement that confirmed her misgivings.

A stocky man darted out the front door, almost falling over Moira's powerchair. *Rutger Milvery,* Moira thought, noting the shock of white hair.

When she leveled her stun-gun at him, Rutger started to run, opting for a circuitous path through the elaborately-landscaped flowerbeds. Moira stabbed at the arm controls, sending the powerchair into hover mode. As the chair gathered speed, she tersely updated Oskar via hands-free.

When Moira's chair drew level with Rutger, he threw up his arms in resignation and stopped abruptly, leaning forward to rest his hands on his knees. Oskar arrived, panting, and snapped the cuffs around Rutger's wrists, reciting their suspect's rights as he did so.

Back in the interrogation room at the precinct, Rutger glared at his captors.

"We think," Moira said quietly, "that you killed Logan Roberts."

Rutger raised and dropped his powerful shoulders in a shrug. "I told you, I was in my dorm unit. Did you check the bioreadouts?"

"Yeah, our IT guy checked them," Oskar said. "Just like in Logan's case, the data was doctored. Someone set up a program to repeat previous data so the readouts would show the room was occupied, even if it wasn't. Program probably got used any time someone wanted to do extra-curricular activity during the evening hours."

"So? That wouldn't prove I *wasn't* there," Rutger said smugly. "Besides, why would I kill Logan?"

"Jealousy." Moira leaned back to watch Rutger's face. *Cool customer, alright.* Though a jaw muscle twitched, Rutger evinced no other signs of discomfort. "You lied to us about not knowing Logan Roberts outside of work."

"So what?" Rutger sounded impatient, belligerently so.

"These photos," Moira continued smoothly, ignoring Rutger's tone, "show that it mattered a lot." She slammed down five images, one by one, where Rutger could see them. When the fifth photo landed on the table, Moira noted Rutger's twitch intensify.

"We believe that this photo"—Oskar leaned forward and pointed to the one that showed Logan, Karina, and Rutger in the stands at the basketball game—"was in a photo projector that you removed from Logan's dorm room. You were likely looking for the money, too, but the search team arrived before you got your hands on it."

"Karina was always nice to us," Rutger said, his voice intense. "Logan, though, he didn't treat her like she deserved. He talked about leaving, jumping the project. I didn't want to see him break her heart."

"Yeah, as if killing her boyfriend wouldn't do the same thing," Moira retorted.

"She wouldn't *look* at me when Logan was around," Rutger said, his face flushing.

"How did you know Eddie Garcia?" Oskar asked.

"I did two jobs for the Syndicate. Logan got me in on it," Rutger replied. "I begged off after that. When the cops found the body, I figured framing Garcia would be a way to muddy the trail." He paused. "I was so close. Another ten minutes and the body would have been gone."

✦ ✦ ✦

"SO LOGAN REALLY had planned to go on the lam," Moira said to Oskar as they began clearing their desks for the day.

"Ironically, they were planning to go within the week, according to Evie." Oskar shook his head. "Logan said he just had some loose ends to clear up."

"Why run? He was headed off-planet soon, if all went well," Akai commented.

"Once in the Syndicate, it's hard to get out," Moira replied. "Logan was afraid that even after he left, they'd still be after Evie. Ironically, he'd repaid her initial loan several times over."

"He and Evie planned to move to the East Coast, get a fresh start," Oskar added.

"Makes sense. There are small towns out there that the syndicates haven't touched. Not worth their while," Akai said, nodding.

"Someone will need to let Elias Huber know that the death wasn't due to external forces trying to sabotage his project," Moira said, her tone thoughtful. "I'll go in person, after I leave here. I have a feeling Mr. Huber is one of those guys who works late."

"Need someone to go with you?" Oskar asked.

"I'm fine," Moira replied. She held her breath for a moment, hoping Oskar wouldn't insist.

"See you tomorrow, then," Oskar said, waving as he headed for the door.

"See you," Moira replied. Her comm device buzzed, and she smiled as she read the message. Elias *was* working late.

Moira pointed her chair in the direction of the elevator and headed to GenAlpha, deep in thought.

Three years after she plummeted head-first into the boards during that fateful playoff game, ending her career as a professional hockey player, Moira had taken up detective work. Aptitude testing had steered her in that direction, although it wasn't something she'd ever before envisioned herself doing.

In spite of that, she'd performed her new role with a competence that both surprised and gratified her. Lately, though, it had started to feel like the same old same-old. But things had been different since her conversation with Elias at Gen-Alpha. She felt excited, open to new possibilities.

I'm not committing, just getting information, Moira reminded herself. Still, she had to admit she *was* tired of working homicide cases. Even if you caught the guilty party, it never brought the dead back.

I'm ready for something new, she thought, surprising herself with the realization. The Precinct had provided her with stability and a certain comfort level for a period of time after her injury. But she was ready for more now. Ready for adventure.

Moira rolled her powerchair into the elevator and pressed

the button for the ground level. As the elevator started to move, she closed her eyes. She was picturing herself riding the wind currents on outspread wings as purple-leaved trees flashed past.

Would there be birds? Mammals? Or some entirely new life forms?

It'd be cool to find out.

Moira smiled as she exited the elevator and piloted her powerchair across the atrium of New Toronto Police Precinct Four, urging the machine to a quicker-than-usual pace. The sooner she got to Gen-Alpha, the better.

A world lay waiting.

Contributors

Victoria Feistner is a writer, a graphic designer, and an artisan in equal parts, although some of those parts are more equal than others. She resides in Toronto with her partner and their two cats. News and examples of her writing can be found at www.victoriafeistner.com.

Yvette Franklin is a beach loving, LA living, cancer surviving writer and editor. She has greatly appreciated her time hanging with the Deaf and Disability communities over many years. In *Dark Space*, the previous Elm science fiction collection from Leonie Skye, she told the story of Sali and Jacksom, and has other stories in various Elm mystery and romance collections. She also gives a big shout out to Don Grushkin for his historical perspective on Deaf culture.

Tim Lamoureux is a writer living in Los Angeles, California. Born in Baton Rouge, he left gators behind to wrangle rattlesnakes in Tucson, Arizona, where he grew up. A Celtic enthusiast, when he's not listening to Tri Yann while sitting in traffic, Tim can be found reading Breton lais to his Maine Coon, Méabh.

David Preyde is a writer who has Asperger's Syndrome and a few other things. He lives in Toronto with his wife and two children: a mutt named Abbey and a toddler named Gwen.

Leonie Skye has short stories in Shimmer, Luna Station Quarterly, and, as Sarah Meacham, Entropy Magazine, as well as linguistics articles in the *Journal of Linguistic Anthropology* and *Mind, Culture, and Activity*. She is the editor of small press Elm Books' science fiction anthologies, *Dark Space* and *Strange Flight*. She lives in Portland, Oregon with her partner, daughter, and chihuahua-corgi person. You can also find her on Twitter @leonie_skye or her website: hazylightwraiths.wordpress.com.

Lisa Timpf is a retired HR and communications professional who lives in Simcoe, Ontario. Her short stories have appeared in a variety of magazines and anthologies, including *New Myths, Outposts of Beyond, Enter the Rebirth, Future Days*, and *The Martian Wave*. You can find out more about Lisa's writing projects by visiting her web site, lisatimpf.blogspot.com.

CPSIA information can be obtained
at www.ICGtesting.com
Printed in the USA
FSHW021128110120
65483FS